TORY'S TUESDAY

by Linda Kay Silva

"I had noticed Elsa the first day I stopped in at her Papa's bakery. From the moment I saw her beautiful, long hair, I knew that I wanted to be with her. I stopped by every day after that, and soon, we became very close. One night, on one of our many evening strolls, we spoke of our dreams of the future, what we wanted to do when we grew up. Suddenly, I bent down and kissed her cheek. It seemed like the most natural thing to do." Marissa backed away from the podium and adjusted her glasses. "It has been natural ever since."

Many of the women in the audience smiled at her naked honesty.

Other Works by Linda Kay Silva

Taken By Storm

TORY'S TUESDAY

by
Linda Kay Silva

PARADIGM
Publishing
Company

Cover Design by Hummingbird Graphics
Book Design and Typesetting by Paradigm Publishing

Printed in the United States by McNaughton and Gunn

Library of Congress Catalog Card Number: 91-66756
ISBN 0-9628595-3-2

Dedicated To

Princess—you walked out of the pages and into my life, bringing so much love and laughter with you. Your friendship, your understanding of who I am, helps me make the music of the night.

Special Thanks To

Mark—for playing sports with me as if I were your little brother and not your little sister. So much of my inner strength and confidence was built when we were kids. Thanks for always believing in me.

Otis, Kristin, and Aunt Cathy—for your support, your love, and, most of all, your familial friendship after *STORM*.

James—for feeding my artistic spirit and sense of adventure.

J.P.—for your rebellious nature, your individualism, your sense of freedom, and your quiet support. I would want to be just like you if either of us ever grows up!

My Students (Past and Present)—for not caring that I'm weird. We have some fun, don't we? Remember, show, don't tell.

Dori, Becky, Marianne, and Karen—you influenced me and my life more than you could possibly know. Thanks just isn't enough.

Chapter One

"My name is Elsa Liebowitz, and I am a survivor of the Auschwitz death camp in Poland." The petite, gray-haired woman paused as a ripple of electricity ran through the young collegiate women in the auditorium. Most were sitting rigidly alert, determined to catch every word from the demure speaker. There was a hum of anticipation, and as it died down, Elsa stepped back up to the microphone. The sea of eager faces reminded her of her youth, when she realized that knowledge wasn't just power, it was survival; when being young and healthy was often the only reason one was kept alive. Ah, but that was before. Before . . .

Looking over at Marissa, her lover of nearly forty years, Elsa smiled. Since they started their speaking engagements over fifteen years ago, Elsa had always been the one to begin. Elsa thought that the telling of their experience would get easier with age, but she was mistaken. The pain, the scars, the horrible memories never faded, never dulled with time. Perhaps, like a picked scab, the wounds would never heal properly. Maybe that's what she and Marissa really were—scab-pickers who reminded the world of the largest, ugliest scar on the face of humanity.

Marissa motioned toward the awaiting crowd. Her face wore the gentle smile that won Elsa's heart all those years ago.

"Go on," she whispered. "They're waiting."

Turning back to the silent crowd, Elsa nodded to them. "Marissa and I are living reminders of the intense cruelty man is capable of inflicting upon himself. We have come here today to share with you our experiences of Nazi Germany, not because we want your pity or sympathy, but to ensure that society never forgets the atrocities that people are capable of." Elsa paused here and scanned the audience. She and Marissa had spoken in Berlin, London, and Paris, but only in the United States did she find such a diversity of nationalities. Women of every size, shape, and color looked up at her with wide, innocent eyes; eyes she recalled seeing in the mirror only days before deportation.

"But before Germany, before the atrocities, I must begin at the beginning, when Marissa and I were two young women about your age. We were two girls of opposing backgrounds who were able to see beyond our parents' labels, beyond Poland's highly prejudiced communities. The year was 1938, and we lived in a little town called Bialystok, about two hundred kilometers outside of Warsaw. I worked in my Papa's bakery, where I met that lovely lady sitting over there." Pride flowed from Elsa as she reached for the hand of the only woman she had ever loved. As she did, her left sleeve slid up her arm, revealing a five digit tattoo.

"Marissa stopped by Papa's bakery every day on her way home from work, and we became fast friends. Well . . . maybe not so fast. For you see, Poland was having a difficult time with its own version of what was called the 'Jewish Dilemma' or the 'Jewish Question.' The nation was divided between Polish nationalists and communists, and neither had much regard for a somewhat large Jewish population. And therein was our first hurdle. While Marissa is of Polish descent, I am a Jew." Elsa waited for a young woman in the back to sit down. *"The second hurdle was my father. While Papa only wanted me to be happy, he did not think it was wise for me to have a Pole for a friend, and we discussed it on several occasions."*

"But, Papa, she is my best friend. She is my only friend."

"She is your only Gentile friend, Elsa. You should not be seen with her. It's bad for the business."

"Bad for the business? Come now, Papa, even a stubborn old goat like you have to admit that she brings in a great deal of business."

Papa waved her off. "That's just it. Why is she not home helping her family?"

"Oh, Papa," Elsa said, wrapping her arms around the old man's neck. He smelled of sugar and flour and was, indeed, the gingerbread man her mother used to call him. "You would not begrudge me of my dearest friend?" Elsa stuck her nose in his ear and knew she had him.

"Since your mother died, you have been impossible to say no to. You wring an old man's heart; you know that don't you?"

Squeezing him, Elsa jumped up and started for the door. "Thank you, Papa! You make me the happiest girl in the world!"

"Bah," he grumbled, waving a doughy hand in the air. "A husband should make you so happy."

Before she opened the door, Elsa stood with arms akimbo. "Papa—"

"I know." The old man bowed his head like a little boy.

"I promised Mutti I would look after you. How can I look after you, Josef, and a husband?"

"I can look out for myself."

It was an old argument, one that weakened with age. As much as her father wanted her to marry, Elsa knew it pained him to think of her leaving. Raising Josef alone and running the bakery was much more than he could possibly handle.

"So can I, Papa. You have taught me well."

"You're not getting any younger."

"Neither are you."

Both stood, arms across their chest, staring at each other.

"You need a man."

"I have you."

"No, no, a husband."

"Then you need a wife." Elsa saw a glimmer of a smile on his wrinkled face.

"You are so much like your mother," he said, shaking his head.

"Is that so bad?"

"Of course not. It makes me love you more."

Elsa hugged him and stepped back to wipe the flour off his chin. "I'm going to see Marissa now."

Nodding his head, her father smiled. "I don't suppose your friend has a man?"

"No, Papa, she doesn't."

"The world is changing, isn't it, Elsa?"

"Yes, Papa, it is."

3

"And so my first obstacle was hurdled." Elsa picked up the glass of water and took a sip. "It would, by no means, be our last conversation on the subject, but at least we had an understanding. I tried to see her away from the bakery so that Papa wouldn't be too nervous. On Tuesdays, we met at a cafe called Tory's, where we would sit outside and talk for hours.

"On this particular Tuesday, Marissa was very solemn. Instead of her usual warming grin and hug, her face bore a frown, and her emerald green eyes looked as if they hadn't closed for sleep in days."

At Tory's, Marissa reached across the table and took Elsa's hands in hers. Marissa's strong square jaw was set, and her eyes narrowed to fine points. For a moment, her posture scared Elsa.

"There is talk, Elsa. Talk of terrible things that are going on between the Germans and the Russians." Marissa leaned across the table and lowered her voice. "Poland is not safe. My . . . friends urge me to take you and leave here before it is too late. They say Hitler is insane and there is talk that he might attack Poland."

"Attack Poland?"

"Shh. It is only speculation now, but our information points in that direction."

Elsa's right hand instinctively clutched her throat. "You mean he would declare war on us?"

Marissa shook her head. "No, not declare, but simply do."

"What will we do?" Elsa had known little about politics or political actions until she met Marissa. Marissa had become her window to a whole different world; a world that was, quite often, very frightening.

"I want you and your family to leave Poland."

"Leave Poland?" Elsa wasn't sure she had heard correctly.

"Keep your voice down."

"Keep my voice down? You sit here and tell me you want me to leave Poland, and you think I should sit here quietly? I most certainly will not." Elsa folded her arms in defiance. "This is crazy talk."

Reaching across the table, Marissa touched the long, brown hair she had grown to love. "These are crazy times."

"You cannot be serious. Leave Poland? Where would we go?"

"Anywhere out of Europe. Someplace far from Hitler's clutches. The world, Elsa, our world, is no longer safe. War threatens all of Europe, and if the Germans and Russians have indeed signed a pact, then all of Poland is in grave danger. You must believe me."

Elsa gazed hard into Marissa's eyes. Her deep, sea-green eyes, which were usually so tender and clear, were misty and hard, as they always became whenever she spoke of Germany.

"I do believe you, Mari, but I can do nothing about it. You know Papa will never leave, and I will never go without him." Elsa bowed her head and gazed at her hands sitting in her lap.

Gently cupping Elsa's chin, Marissa lifted her face and smiled kindly into it. "And I would not expect you to. But we must get your Papa, Josef, and you out of Poland. Europe is not safe for Jews. We must convince your Papa of that."

"It would be easier to ask the sun to drop out of the sky."

Marissa's smile widened. "Perhaps, but we must try."

"But what of you? Surely you would come?"

"Of course. If you think I would let you out of my sight for too long, you do not know me as well as you should."

"But I do."

Marissa grinned. "Then it's settled. As soon as we can convince your father, we'll get you out of here?"

Elsa nodded and swallowed hard. The sun, it seemed, would never fall out of the sky, yet Marissa was willing to bet that it would.

If only she had half of Marissa's strength.

Chapter Two

Taking another sip of water, Elsa moved over to where Marissa was sitting, and the two exchanged warm smiles.

"You get better every time, my love," Marissa said, patting Elsa's hand as they exchanged places.

Marissa stood in front of the podium calm and erect. Her long, blonde hair was in a ponytail that hung loosely past her shoulders. Large, clear-rimmed glasses sat perched on her nose, and a silver medallion hung on her slender neck. At a glance, she appeared forty or fifty, but not sixty. Her skin was smooth, absent of the wrinkles many her age carry with them, and her green eyes were alive with energy and brilliance. Scanning the audience appraisingly, she stepped up to the microphone. Much taller than Elsa, she had to adjust the mike before speaking.

"I am Marissa Kowalski, and I, too, am here to share our experience. But our story isn't one of only horror and atrocities. It is also of love, courage, and hope. It is one that I believe portrays the power of love and the near invincibility of those who have faith in that love." Marissa paused here to glance over at Elsa. After all these years, she still found her to be the most beautiful woman in the room.

"We cannot continue or even try to tell our story without first conveying the importance of our then out-of-bounds relationship. We fell in love so quickly we did not have time to see our differences or," Marissa chuckled, "our alikeness." Marissa looked over to Elsa again and grinned. Decades of love flowed between the two women.

"I had noticed Elsa the first day I stopped in at her Papa's bakery. From the moment I saw her beautiful, long hair, I knew that I wanted to be with her. I stopped by every day after that, and soon, we became very close. One night, on one of our many evening strolls, we spoke of our dreams of the future, what we wanted to do when we grew up. Suddenly, I bent down and kissed her cheek. It seemed like the most natural thing to do." Marissa backed away from the podium and adjusted her glasses. "It has been natural ever since."

Many of the women in the audience smiled at her naked honesty.

"I was a seamstress at the time and was designing and sewing many of my own dresses. While I did not live with my family, I did send them money when I could make it. And when the economic condition of Poland was at its worst, I was still able to make money."

"What's in the box?" Josef asked Marissa as she set a three-foot box on the counter.

"It's a surprise for your sister."

Josef's face fell.

"But I brought you something as well, little man." Reaching into her pocket, Marissa produced two cat's eye marbles.

"Wow! Cat's eyes! I lost mine to that David Rich. He cheats."

Marissa smiled. At nine years old, Josef was one of the most responsible people Marissa had ever met. He could work the bakery almost as well as his Papa and cooked better than most women Marissa knew.

"That's what I've heard. Now don't lose these to him. They're the last ones I have."

"I won't. From now on, when I play with him, I'll use my crummy marbles." As Josef scurried up the stairs to get his sister, Marissa nodded her hello to Elsa's father.

"Business good?"

"Been better. Elsa is upstairs doing the books. Care for a roll or something?"

Before she could answer, Elsa bounded down the stairs. Her hair hung loosely down her shoulders, and she wore a smile that nearly touched both ears.

"Josef said you brought me a present."

Pushing the box toward Elsa, Marissa grinned sheepishly.

"Let's take it upstairs." Grabbing the box in one hand and Marissa's wrist in the other, Elsa went upstairs and into her room.

"I love your surprises!" Clapping her hands together, Elsa gazed down at the box and then back at Marissa.

7

"Open it, Sweetness."

Pulling the top off the box, Elsa reached in and carefully pulled a turquoise and black dress out. The folds of the dress fell silently as she held it up to look at it.

"Oh, Mari . . ." Burying her face in the neckline, Elsa inhaled deeply. "It's beautiful."

Marissa stood next to her and stroked her hair. "So are you."

Holding it out again to look at it, Elsa shook her head. "It must have taken you days."

"More like weeks. It's one of my originals."

"Has Madame seen it?"

"No. I was afraid she would want it."

Elsa held the dress in one hand and caressed Marissa's cheek with the back of her hand. "And well she would have. This is your best yet."

Kissing Elsa's hand, Marissa nodded. "And that is precisely why it should belong to you, and you alone. Try it on." Stepping behind Elsa, Marissa untied her apron and slowly slid her dress off her shoulders. Dropping tiny kisses on her bare shoulders, Marissa reached around her waist and ran her hand along her taut stomach. The heat rose between Marissa's legs and seemed to travel to her fingertips as they glided across her creamy skin. It always amazed her that Elsa could stay slim working around so many pastries.

"You taste so delicious," Marissa said, biting Elsa's naked shoulder and exposed neck. Elsa could move her to passion she did not know was possible. "Let me help you try it on."

Squirming playfully away, Elsa turned to face Marissa. "You have other things on your mind, I'm afraid."

Marissa's eyes danced from the dress to Elsa's body and back again. "Perhaps. Does that bother you?"

Elsa blushed. "Of course not. You make my head spin, Mari."

Sweeping Elsa up in her arms, Marissa kissed her passionately. "I'd rather spin your heart, Sweetness."

8

"Oh, you do. Now will you help me with this dress before Josef or Papa wonder what we're up to?"

Pulling the dress over her slip, Elsa backed into Marissa so she could help button it. Sashaying over to the mirror, Elsa studied herself in a variety of poses.

"Oh, Mari, it's incredible."

Threading her arms around Elsa's waist, Marissa rubbed her face against Elsa's hair. "I'm glad you like it."

"Like it? I love it. Thank you so much." Hearing the creak of the stairs, Elsa quickly pulled away.

"You make that dress stunning, my love. It looks wonderful on you."

Before Elsa could respond, Josef's voice drifted upstairs.

"Elsie," came Josef's voice in the hall. "Papa needs you downstairs."

"Tell him I'm coming, Josef." Quickly stripping off the dress, Elsa carefully placed it back in the box. "Come for dinner?"

Marissa nodded and kissed Elsa's ear. "And dessert?"

"Mari!" Pushing her away, Elsa blushed. "The things you say—"

"Are a direct result of the things you do," Marissa said in a low voice.

Elsa slowly backed away and blushed. "I must help Papa. Thank you for the beautiful dress."

"Thank you, my love, for wearing it so grandly. I could sew a horse blanket for you to wear and you would make it look like a queen's robe."

"You are such a sweetheart. Come to dinner at eight." Starting down the stairs, Elsa turned one last time. "I love you," she whispered. Then she turned and was gone.

Chapter Three

Marissa paused while another latecomer sat down in the auditorium. "I learned how to sew when I was just a small child. My mother taught me her trade before she died. Little did she know at the time, my ability with the needle and thread would save my life.

"I worked in a tiny shop in town, for a woman I simply knew as Madame. Madame loved my designs, and whenever I created a new one, she would often buy the design and the dress and ship it somewhere. I knew she was making a good profit off them because every now and then she would press a coin into my hand. Soon, I realized she was sending my dresses to Paris and Berlin, where only the very rich could afford them. How she managed that, I did not know."

Marissa carried a coat box under her arm and waved to Elsa who sat at their usual table at Tory's.

"Another?" Elsa asked, eyeing the box.

Marissa shook her head. "Sorry. Madame already has a buyer for this one." Opening the box, Marissa proudly held up the red dress for Elsa to see.

"Where does she find such beautiful material at times like these?"

Replacing the lid, Marissa sat down and frowned. "I don't know, and I won't ask. She has connections somewhere. It's best to leave it alone."

Elsa nodded. "Who do you suppose buys them?"

Marissa shrugged. "People with a lot of money."

"I get compliments on my turquoise dress all the time."

"And well you should. You look beautiful in it."

Suddenly, the smile left Elsa's face, and she leaned across the table to hold Marissa's hands.

"I overheard two gentlemen talking in the shop today, and they said that Hitler continues to rave about the

Jewish problem. Does he honestly believe we are at fault for his country's difficulties?"

Marissa nodded. "I'm afraid Poland isn't the only country tramping on the Jews. Your people seem to rub the hair backward on much of Eastern Europe."

"It frightens me. They said that Hitler hopes to turn the world against us. Is that true?"

Squeezing Elsa's cold hands, Marissa moved closer. "The Nazi Party is trying to rally the German people. The easiest way to do that is to rise against a common evil."

"Common evil! Mari, how can you say such a thing?"

"It's no secret that the Jews are perceived as threats. Hitler has chosen to take this perception and use it as a means of manipulating the masses. It has been very successful thus far."

Elsa withdrew her hands and crossed her arms. The frown lines around her eyes creased as she stared out over the plaza.

"You believe Hitler will start another world war, don't you?"

Marissa nodded. "My friends in the Resistance say it is only a matter of time. Look at what he has done to Austria and the Sudetenland. No one is stopping him."

"Surely the Americans won't allow it."

This made Marissa laugh. Elsa, in her protected little bakery, was so naive. Like many of her friends, she tried to bury her head in the present conditions of Poland instead of looking at the bigger world picture. She did not want Elsa to be so naive as to think that all was well when, clearly, it wasn't.

"Don't count on the Americans or anyone else to save Europe from that madman. We must protect ourselves or—"

"Or?"

Marissa lowered her voice. "Or we will find ourselves in the same leaking boat as the Austrians."

For a moment, the two young women sat in silence, each listening to their own fear creeping around in the attic of their consciousness.

"Mari?" Elsa said at last.

"Yes?"

"If Hitler attacks us, will we be ready?"

Taking Elsa's hand, Marissa held it tightly. "I don't know, Sweetness. I honestly don't know."

Chapter Four

"In September of 1939, Hitler did indeed attack Poland, starting World War II. Bombs rained down on Bialystok and many other non-military targets. But the occurrences that happened shortly after defeating us were just the beginning of the nightmare. Jews were driven from their homes to the larger cities, and Jewish businesses were destroyed and ransacked. To contain the Jews, Hitler built ghettos, where he confined the inhabitants within the walls of the city. Under German occupation, the Polish people were starved, beaten, physically and sexually abused, and had no rights. In every town the Germans occupied, Kristallnacht (Crystal Night) was relived until the Jewish people could do nothing but live in terror. When they began deporting Jews to work camps, I knew I had to get Elsa and her family away from the ghetto."

Gathering a handful of pebbles, Marissa tossed them at the window to the left of the bakery and waited.

"It's me," Marissa whispered in the darkness, when a small beam of light came through the window.

"I'll be right down."

As Marissa waited, she could hear the German patrols marching through the street. It was long past curfew, but Marissa knew the back streets well enough to move through the night unnoticed.

When Elsa opened the door, Marissa crept in and flew into her embrace once the door was closed securely behind them.

"What is it, Mari? Are you alright?"

Pulling away, Marissa nodded. "I am. But you and your family are not. We must leave here tomorrow night. There is a village to the east—"

"I cannot leave. You know as much."

Marissa was firm. "Elsa, have you not seen what the Germans are capable of doing now? Every day they are deporting more and more Jews and Poles alike."

"I will not hear it."

Marissa grabbed Elsa's arm. "You must hear me. The Germans are telling people that they are being deported to special work camps, when, in reality, they are death camps—"

Elsa pried Marissa's hand off her arm. "Camps?"

"Prisons. Horrible, dirty places where the Nazis work people to death. Jews from all over Poland are being deported to these camps." Marissa took Elsa in her arms and hugged her tightly. "My friends in the underground have secured a way for us to leave here tomorrow night. You must have your father and Josef ready by midnight."

Elsa pulled back and reached up to touch Marissa's face. "And if Papa won't come?"

Looking away, Marissa exhaled loudly. "Then you and Josef must leave him."

"No. I cannot. I promised Mutti—"

Marissa turned quickly. "What? That you would put you and your brother in danger because your Papa is too stubborn to see the danger right before his face?" Marissa's voice was cold and hard. She had never spoken to Elsa like this before, but fear motivated her now to cut through the tenderness which had been unsuccessful.

"How will you take care of him if you are deported? What happens if they send you to different camps? He is old—"

"Stop!" Elsa turned and covered her ears. "You are frightening me."

Marissa embraced her once more. "It is a frightening situation. The Nazis are moving us en masse to places far away from here. If we escape, we can head to the smaller villages that have yet to be rounded up. But, we must act quickly."

"And if he won't come?"

"Then you must leave him behind. For Josef's sake."

Elsa's eyes filled with tears. "But Josef is only nine. Surely they wouldn't—"

Marissa's face hardened. "A nine-year-old Jew is still a Jew, Elsa. He must come with you."

14

Lowering her face into Marissa's neck, Elsa barely nodded. She could not bear to think of any harm coming to Josef. He was just a child. "We will be ready. When shall we leave?"

"We leave tomorrow night."

"But we didn't. We had acted too late."

Chapter Five

As Elsa moved to the podium, Marissa stood in front of her and smiled. The years had not diminished the love and admiration they held for each other, and even in a roomful of people, Marissa could gaze into Elsa's face and see nothing but her own love reflecting back.

"Mari," Elsa whispered, trying to get by. "Stop."

Marissa smiled. "Never, my love."

Sitting down in the seat Elsa vacated, Marissa leaned back and gazed at Elsa's still slim figure. Elsa could still rouse a passion in her equal to what she felt decades ago. Night after night in the camp, she would replay her favorite love-making memory in her mind. Even in a crowded auditorium, Marissa's mind easily drifted back to the memory that kept her going when it seemed like life had come to an end.

Taking the hairbrush from Elsa's hand, Marissa stroked the long, wavy locks hanging like a satin curtain down her back. She loved Elsa's hair; the silky way it fell over her body and face when they were in bed, and the soft, silent swish it made when she flipped it over her shoulder.

"That feels wonderful," Elsa whispered, closing her eyes and tilting her head back while Marissa slowly pulled the brush through Elsa's thick mane.

"You look wonderful." Running her hand through Elsa's hair, Marissa marvelled at its softness. "You have the most beautiful hair of any woman I have ever seen."

"You always say that," Elsa said, smiling.

"Are you tired of hearing it already, my love?" Setting the brush down, Marissa pulled both hands through the wavy mass until she could collect it all in one hand. Holding Elsa's hair up and away from her shoulders, Marissa bent down and lightly kissed the back of Elsa's neck.

A low murmur was Elsa's only response.

Moving her mouth down Elsa's neck, Marissa paused at the soft spot where her slender neck joined her small shoulders. As always, Elsa smelled like a butter cookie rolled in cinnamon as the fragrances of the bakery lingered about her.

Mouth still poised on Elsa's soft shoulders, Marissa slowly pulled the nightgown away from her skin, dropping it silently to the floor.

"Mari . . .," Elsa moaned, pressing herself against Marissa.

Letting go of the bundle of hair, Marissa lightly brushed both hands down Elsa's bare chest and arms, grinning as her fingertips slid over the goose bumps brought on by her caresses. Hands gliding around the small, pert breasts, Marissa was careful to avoid the nipples she knew were aching to be touched.

Nuzzling Elsa's hair with her face, Marissa softly whispered. "I wish to make love with you, Sweetness."

Reaching her arm over her head, Elsa pressed the back of Marissa's head deeper into her hair. "Mmmm. I would love you to." Turning to face Marissa, but remaining seated, Elsa gazed up into the dazzling, green eyes longing for her. "Your eyes give away your desire."

Looking down at her, Marissa ran her index finger from Elsa's forehead down to her nose, her chin, her cleavage, until it came to rest in the middle of her stomach. "Then they must tell you how deeply I want you."

Elsa nodded as she stood, drawing Marissa closer. "Papa and Josef will be gone all afternoon. There is no hurry."

Marissa nodded. The heat from Elsa's body radiated as if it were an open oven, driving Marissa's passion faster beneath her chest. She could feel Elsa's desire and sensed her need to give herself to her. Cupping Elsa's chin in her hand, Marissa pulled her forward until their lips ever-so-lightly touched. The soft, teasing way her tongue ran over Elsa's mouth stoked the flames burning within each of them.

From their embrace, Elsa slightly withdrew so her fingers could undo the buttons on Marissa's blouse. As her tiny hands pushed back the dark blue blouse, Elsa let out a gasp.

"Mari! You . . . you're not wearing a br—"

Marissa smiled wryly. "You don't find it appealing?"

The mask of surprise vanished as quickly as it had come; a sly grin was a shadow across Elsa's face. "You are wicked." Pause. "But I must admit—"

Marissa tossed her head back and laughed. "I thought as much." Pulling Elsa to her, Marissa kissed her long and hard, never letting Elsa pull away.

At last, when Elsa did pull away, she threw back the covers to her bed and brought Marissa to her. "Come here, you shameless tart," Elsa said, opening her arms for Marissa.

Dropping her skirt on the floor before she got in, Marissa gently laid on top of her much smaller lover. Beneath her, Elsa's skin was hot next to hers, already creating a small stream of sweat between them. Laying her mouth over Elsa's, Marissa delighted in their sweet softness. Nibbling her bottom lip, her tongue slowly explored Elsa's teeth and tongue before returning to bite and tease her bottom lip. Allowing her hands to roam freely over the silkiness of Elsa's body, Marissa felt Elsa's undulating hips reaching for more than just her teasing pressure.

"Mari—"

"Plenty of time, Sweetness," Marissa answered, circling around and around Elsa's breasts with her fingertips. Trying to ignore her own heat rising like a mirage on a hot desert road, Marissa removed her tongue from Elsa's mouth and slowly drew a straight, wet line with it to the hard tip of Elsa's chocolate brown nipple.

"Please—" Elsa moaned, arching her back, pressing herself against Marissa's nakedness.

Taking the nipple in her mouth, Marissa swirled it around in her mouth, flicking her tongue back and forth across it. With every movement, Elsa's breathing quickened, and her body arched and pressed. Taking the other chocolate drop between her fingers, Marissa played with both nipples until Elsa could no longer stand it.

Rolling over so that she was now on top of Marissa, Elsa moved her hips rhythmically into Marissa. A drop of sweat rolled down her stomach as she pressed their bodies together. Taking her own breast and sliding it into Marissa's mouth, Elsa moved up and down Marissa's body, arching her back whenever Marissa would take her nipple between her teeth and roll it back and forth.

"Ohhh," Elsa moaned, pulling her breast away and plunging her tongue into Marissa's awaiting mouth. "You are making me crazy."

Turning Elsa over to her side, Marissa ran her hand up and down the soft inside of her thigh as her mouth continued to move in sync with Elsa's passion. Gently pushing her legs apart, Marissa caressed the soft, wet hair and smooth skin of Elsa's thigh. She had never been as excited as she was at this moment and tried to block out her own eagerness, her own pent up desires.

Taking one of Elsa's breasts in her mouth, Marissa slowly entered Elsa with two fingers. A low, guttural sound came from Elsa's throat as she lifted her hips into the air.

"Now, Mari. Please, now!"

Rolling on top of Elsa, Marissa kissed her with hard, passionate desire as her hand caressed the tender places she knew would bring Elsa to climax.

As their bodies dipped and rose together, Marissa felt her own pulsating rhythm spring to life between her legs. She could not and did not want to stop it as Elsa moved her hips and legs against Marissa's own heated fervor.

At once, Elsa gripped the sheets and arched her back for one long, continuous moment as her body succumbed to the undulations and stimulation of her lover. At once, Marissa felt her own body explode and her muscles tense as Elsa's driving heat edged her over the peak.

At last, when the pulsing sensation slowly subsided, Elsa lowered herself back to the bed as Marissa crawled on top of her, sweaty and spent.

"Oh, how you must love me, Marissa Kowalski," Elsa murmured, wrapping her arms around Marissa's naked shoulders. "Give me a moment, my love, and I will show you just how much I love you back."

Closing her eyes, Marissa nestled into Elsa's breast and fell fast asleep.

Chapter Six

Readjusting the mike to suit her short height, Elsa continued. "I was already up when they first beat on the door to the bakery. Unable to sleep after my late-night visit with Marissa, I had been up packing and unpacking, trying to figure out just what one brings when escaping into the countryside. The only thing I seemed to know for sure was that I would wear the turquoise dress Mari had made me."

When the rapping started, Elsa's father promptly marched down the stairs and whipped open the door. Perhaps it was the fact that his shop was allowed to remain open that gave him the courage to act imposed upon. Whatever the reason, her Papa acted like a man who did not understand that his country had been occupied.

"What do you want?" he demanded in Polish.

One of the young officers dressed in his polished black uniform pushed past him. "You have five minutes to get your valuables together, Herr Liebowitz." The soldier spoke in German, which most Poles living in the ghetto quickly picked up.

"I will not."

Just then, Elsa and Josef ran down the stairs, in time to see the officer backhand her father, sending him crashing against the glass display.

"Papa!" little Josef cried, running to the officer and kicking him.

"Damned little Jew brat," the officer said, striking Josef on the forehead.

"Josef! Papa!" Elsa immediately knelt at her father's side. "Papa, are you alright?"

"I am fine," muttered, pulling himself to his feet. "These Nazi pigs cannot have my bakery!"

Elsa fearfully glanced up at the officer, afraid he may have understood her father's harsh words.

"But, Papa, it is too late. You must do as they say. Go upstairs now and pack your things. Josef, you, too."

"Where are we going?" Josef asked, rubbing his forehead.

"Just do as I say, both of you." Rising, Elsa turned to the officer standing at the door with his arms crossed. "Where are you taking us?" she asked in her best German.

"You have three minutes," he answered in German.

"Josef, take Papa upstairs and help him pack." Trying to keep her hands from trembling, Elsa went into the back of the bakery and opened the tiny safe hidden among the bread baskets. Taking as many bills as she could manage, she stuffed them in her shoe.

"My word," she uttered, peering out the back window. Hundreds of her fellow townspeople were being rounded up. Everything Marissa had warned her about had come to pass. Old and young, Jew and Gentile alike, were being herded like cattle down the road toward the train station. Clutching their few precious possessions, families huddled together for support.

Soon enough, Elsa thought, she and her small family would join the throngs of people making their way down the cobblestone street to unknown destinations. Were they going to those horrible places Marissa had warned them of? Elsa shuddered at the thought.

Glancing into the bakery, she saw the two soldiers stuffing their faces with the day-old pastries. Reaching over her head, Elsa pulled the old, splintered ladder down and climbed up into Josef's room.

"Josef," she whispered, startling the boy.

"Elsie, he will not pack. He just sits." Josef's wide-eyed stare was like that of a deer about to be run over by a train.

"Let him sit then. Are you packed?"

Josef nodded.

"Good boy. Now I need you to go find Marissa. Here." Handing Josef the rest of the money, Elsa backed down the ladder, followed by her brother.

"But I cannot leave now. Papa needs us."

Elsa smiled warmly at him and rustled his hair. "And we need Marissa. She will be able to tell us what is going on. Now go. And if anyone stops you, use the money. But do not stop until you find her. Hurry!" Watching Josef run out the side door, Elsa pushed the ladder back up and walked into the bakery where the soldiers stood licking apple fritter guts off their fingers.

"*Schnell, Fraulein,*" the taller one commanded. "*Mach schnell!*"

Nodding politely, Elsa ran up the stairs and found her father sitting on his bed holding his head in his hands.

"Papa, come on! You will only anger them."

Not looking up, he only shook his head sadly. "What have I done? You and Marissa tried to warn me that it would come to this, but I thought . . . because the bakery was open . . . Oh, Elsa, I have been such a fool. What would your mother have thought?"

Kneeling in front of him, Elsa took his hands in hers. "She would say that now is the time for all of us to stick together. Josef and I need you, Papa. You must be strong."

He gazed down at her, eyes weary and red. "Strong as when your mother died?"

Elsa swallowed. "No, Papa. Stronger."

Marissa stepped back up to the mike as Elsa finished. The strain of the memory showing visibly on Elsa's face, Marissa put her arm around Elsa's waist and pulled her close.

"I ran into young Josef only blocks from the bakery. He managed to reach me to tell me what I already knew. Silently, I cursed myself for being so lenient with Elsa all those months ago. But there was no time for regrets. With Josef in one hand and my bag in the other, we silently made our way to the first living hell we would experience during our lengthy ordeal: the trains."

Lugging Josef in her right hand and fending off the gypsies and the starving with the other, Marissa made her way to the train station.

"Elsie and Papa will be there, too?"

"Yes, Josef, they will." Frantically searching the large crowd, Marissa was relieved to see Elsa and her father at one of the far platforms.

"Elsa!" Marissa cried, hugging her tightly. "Are you okay?"

Elsa nodded. "I am, but I am afraid Papa is not."

Looking over at Elsa's father, who was leaning against a pole, Marissa winced. He had aged ten years overnight. There was a void in his eyes that said he had given up. Like so many others, he had refused to see the signs or heed the warnings. And now, he felt the burden come crashing down on him as his family awaited deportation.

Suddenly, Josef tugged on Marissa's sleeve. "But, Marissa, where are the real trains?"

Focusing only on the people of her village, Marissa had not noticed the long line of box cars waiting like a dinosaur on the track.

Elsa's hand reached for Marissa's. "Mari, they're putting us in cattle cars."

"This can't be," someone behind them whispered.

"Mari?"

Without looking at Elsa, Marissa inhaled slowly and nodded. "I'm afraid this is only the beginning."

Chapter Seven

The hot, cramped boxcars reeked of sweat, urine, defecation, and rancid vomit. Packed too tightly to even sit down, only those on the sides could get fresh air from the slim cracks in the wood.

As the train rambled on, some would call out the name of a town if they could manage to read a sign or see any familiar sights. From the first few names, it was clear to Elsa they were headed south.

"Are they taking us out of Poland?" she asked Marissa.

Marissa shook her head. "I don't think so."

Hours went by without any stop to urinate or drink water, and soon, screaming and moaning could be heard from the other cars. The summer heat seemed to trap the stench inside, making it difficult to breathe. On the other side of the car, a woman was screaming that her baby had died in her arms. They were packed so tight no one could do anything for either her or the baby. Marissa felt Elsa's hand in hers, clenching tightly, afraid that even in the packed car they would somehow get separated.

Several hours later, the tortuous train ride slowly ground to a halt. As the soldiers opened the doors, people tumbled out like toys falling from a child's overstuffed closet. People were clawing and gasping for fresh air as they shielded their eyes from the harsh sunlight. Some pleaded for water, while others tried immediately to run for the bushes. All the while, the soldiers were beating people to the ground and stomping on any who got in their way.

After helping her father off the train, Elsa was amazed at how brittle he suddenly became. In the course of hours, the life seemed to seep out of him and fall to the ground. His shadow was more animated than he. Looking at Elsa and Josef, he stared at them as if he didn't know who they were.

"Papa, we're here." Elsa said, forcing a smile.

Staring at her through empty eyes, he asked, "Where is here?"

Elsa looked over at Marissa, who shrugged. The last name called out was hours ago, and it was Czestochowa.

"Did you lock up the store?" he asked, gazing down at Josef.

"Papa," Elsa said, alarmed. "The store doesn't matter anymore. We're all that matters."

Shaking his head, the old man started to walk away. "I never should have left. Who will watch the store?"

"Papa!" This came from Josef. "Stop it! You're scaring me."

Bending down, Elsa held Josef. "Shh, my little love. There's no need to be afraid. I won't let anything happen to you." As she said this, the soldiers roused everyone together, beating any who did not comply, and formed them into a single file.

"Elsie, are we in Germany now?" Josef, who had not let go of Elsa since they arrived, still clung to her hand.

Elsa smiled down at Josef, who had also seemed to suddenly age. No longer was he a child. In the midst of all the misery and mistreatment, Josef managed to act less like a child and more like a man.

"No, Josef, we are still in Poland." Elsa's eyes grew wide as she saw three soldiers beating the woman who would not give up her dead baby.

"Elsie—"

"Shush, Josef. Do not draw attention to us." This came from Marissa, who had been watching the long line formed ahead of them.

"What is happening, Mari?"

Marissa shook her head. "There is a Nazi in the front of the crowd who seems to be telling everyone where to go."

Elsa felt fear wrap its bony tentacle around her. "Surely they will not separate us?"

Marissa squeezed Elsa's hand. "I do not know. But the people who are fighting it are being beaten and kicked." Turning Elsa around so they were facing each other, Marissa's face was grim. "No matter which way they tell us to go, Elsa, do not fight it. Just do as they say." Then bending down, she grabbed Josef by the shoulders. "Do you hear me, my little man?"

Josef straightened his back. "I do."

Marissa smiled at his bravery. "Did you bring your cat's eyes?"

Josef nodded.

"Do not lose them to another David Rich, okay?"

"Never." Suddenly, Josef handed one to Marissa. "Keep this for good luck."

Marissa took it and grinned. "You are very brave."

Josef grinned. "I'm not afraid."

"I'm glad. You stay that way." Rising, Marissa saw the look in Elsa's eyes and put her arm around her.

"Mari, do you see the people who are being sent over there?"

Marissa looked. The similarities between those in the line did not go unnoticed.

As Elsa stared at the crowd being beaten and shoved away from the line, she noticed it was largely made up of elderly men and women as well as young children and the physically handicapped. Instinctively, she brought Josef closer to her.

"Do not worry, Elsie. I am not afraid."

As Elsa and Josef stepped up to the immaculately dressed officer, Elsa found that she could not look at him. His eyes were cold and evil. With a flick of his wrist, he sent Josef to the group with the children and Elsa to the other.

"Josef!"

"Don't," Marissa growled at her as a heavyset female guard pushed Elsa to the other grouping.

Next was Marissa's turn. The thin man wearing black leather gloves smiled at her.

"Pole?" he said, motioning to her with his head.

"Yes."

"Very good," he said, eyeing her breasts. "Welcome to Auschwitz." As a sinister grin crept over his face, he motioned for Marissa to join Elsa's side of the line.

"Mari!" Elsa cried, running to her and clasping her arms around her neck. "Josef—"

"Shush, Elsa. Those who make noise feel the length of the whip. Do not bring one upon us."

Watching Josef being shoved into the crowd, Elsa felt her heart leap into her throat.

"Elsie!" Josef cried, struggling against the large pair of hands holding him back. "Don't leave me!"

Elsa looked pleadingly at Marissa, who shook her head. "Don't."

When her Papa was violently shoved into the group with Josef, Elsa could no longer contain herself.

"Papa!" she cried, moving across the line and past the guard.

"Elsa, don't! They will hurt you."

"I don't care! Papa!"

Out of nowhere, a sleek, black baton struck Elsa in the stomach, knocking her back into Marissa's arms.

"*Nein, nein, nein!*" the Nazi officer screamed in Elsa's face, hitting her once more.

"Where are they taking them?" Elsa cried, doubling over against the pain.

Marissa grabbed Elsa's arm. "Elsa, you must let them go."

"No! Josef! Let go of my Josef!" Still struggling against Marissa's embrace, Elsa cried out one last time as the group headed down a wide gravel path. Josef turned around one last time and waved to Elsa before being swallowed in the crowd once more.

"I will take care of Papa, Elsie!" Josef yelled before being pushed around the corner and out of sight.

"Oh, Mari," Elsa sobbed, burying her face in Marissa's shoulder. "Where are they going? What are we doing here?"

Wrapping her arms around Elsa, Marissa saw an extremely large guard moving toward them like a shark in the ocean.

"Come, Elsa, we must go with the others. There is nothing we can do for Josef and your Papa. We must take care of ourselves."

Stumbling into the crowd, Elsa turned and watched helplessly as a female guard ripped a child out of the arms of its mother and handed it to another guard. When the woman screamed and ran after the guard, she was struck down and kicked in the head. To her left, two guards were furiously kicking a woman who had grabbed the guards' legs in order to prevent them from taking her twins away.

As she watched in horror, she saw the neatly dressed officer walk up to the woman and smile before raising his gun and shooting her in the face.

"Mari, what is happening?" Elsa's eyes grew wide as a demented mixture of violence and chaos swirled around her like a dust cloud.

"Stay next to me, Elsa," she heard Marissa say, but Elsa was not listening. Her eyes were riveted to the gruesome scene before her. Guards in black uniforms were swinging clubs and whipping Poles, Jews, Czechs, and gypsies around the large receiving center. All around her, people were shouting, screaming, cursing, crying, and bleeding. It was as if hell had ascended to earth. Glancing up at a sign two other Polish women were pointing to, she saw the German words, "*Arbeit Macht Frei.*"

"Work makes you free," Elsa muttered to herself, turning back to Marissa. "Mari, what is this place? Is this one of those work camps?"

Marissa nodded. "I think so."

"Do you think they have a bakery?"

Marissa looked down at Elsa and shook her head sadly. "No, Sweetness. It isn't that kind of work. This is hard labor."

As the guards brusquely herded the women into a large warehouse, Elsa grabbed Marissa's arm and clung to her. Women who had been separated from their families were crying and being told to shut up by two trollish guards.

"Mari?" Elsa whispered, moving closer to her. "Is this where we get our things back? They told us—"

"Elsa, forget what they told you. From now on, never believe anything the Nazis say."

"But—"

"But nothing, my love. Don't you see? Nothing is as they said it would be. There is no food here. This isn't a pleasant work place; it is a labor camp, and we are prisoners now. Prisoners."

Elsa stood up straight and threw her head back. "Prisoners." The images of what had just happened to the other women who fought the guards rang like a bell in her mind. In the far recesses of her mind, the word banged loudly at the door of her inner strength. So loud was it, she almost couldn't hear it above the clanging sound of her own fear. So powerful was it, she could feel the word as it tore its way through her captured spirit.

As Elsa stared hard at the sagging features of the stodgy guards, she understood exactly what she was.

A prisoner.

A prisoner in someone else's war.

Chapter Eight

"How did a Jew bitch like yourself get a dress like this?" The paunchy guard hissed the last syllable in Elsa's face like an angry cobra.

"A friend of mine made—"

"Silence!" The woman squinted her already beady eyes and frowned. "Then you did not buy it, Jewess?"

"No, ma'am. It . . . was a present."

The guard seemed to consider this a moment before nodding.

All around her, women were shedding their clothes, having their glasses ripped off their faces, and taking their shoes off on demands from the guards. Many women refused to take their wedding rings off, but threats of having their fingers cut off prompted them to follow orders.

"I see," the guard said, jerking her head to the dress so another guard would take a look. "Take it off."

Elsa balked, but felt Marissa's grip on her arm.

"Off?"

"Now." The guard's mouth slid into an ugly curl. "All of you, off with your clothes! *Jetzt! Schnell!*"

As the dress fell around her knees, Elsa felt her own courage slipping as well. Naked women stood, pitifully covering up portions of their bodies, while certain ill-dressed women in striped uniforms wearing yellow armbands swooped the clothing off the floor and tossed it into great big bins. When the woman wearing the armband bent to pick up Elsa's dress, the guard cracked her whip.

"No! That one goes to the wives," she ordered, swiping the dress off the ground herself.

"But it's mine," Elsa heard herself say.

Before she could retract her words, the guard's stick came crashing into her stomach once more. As Elsa keeled over, one hand on the floor, the woman raised a fist and brought it violently down on her back.

"The only thing that is yours, Jew bitch, is the skin on your bones. And even that is mine if you get out of line again. Never forget that." Whirling around, the guard left Elsa gasping on her hands and knees.

"Elsa," Marissa whispered, helping Elsa to her feet. "It is only a dress."

"It was a gift from you."

Marissa shook her head. "Elsa, the only gift we have now is that we are together. Nothing else really matters."

Watching as the guards piled their skimpy belongings into a huge pile, Elsa shuddered. Gone were Mrs. Rich's pearl necklace, Anna Freedman's fur coat, and Mrs. Prystowski's leather boots. Gone were the silly trinkets everyone brought along for good luck. And gone, almost painfully so, was her dress from Marissa. The only thing she owned now was her soul, and even then, she wasn't sure that was true.

Chapter Nine

Once they were removed from the room where their clothes were left, the women were forced into another room where rows of single chairs were lined up. Immediately, the German women started issuing orders to each other and the others around them, and in the hustle of the crowd, Marissa and some other Bialystok women were ushered into a different room.

When Elsa turned around to say something to Marissa, she was brutally shoved into the room and forced to sit in one of the chairs.

"Mari!" she cried, only to receive a hard cuff to the side of her head. Turning frantically in the chair, Elsa's heart quickened when Marissa was nowhere to be seen. Hadn't she been behind her when they pushed Elsa into the room? Braving the violence once more, Elsa yelled Marissa's name.

"Silence!" the trolling guard yelled, cracking Elsa's cheek with the back of her hand.

She wanted to stand up and look around for her lover, but the pain and the buzzing in her hears reminded her it was not wise. Where had Marissa gone? Why didn't she at least answer? The woman towering over her seemed to be waiting like a vulture hovering over a dying animal, waiting for the slightest reason to hit her. But Elsa had been hit enough. Wherever Marissa was, she would be sure to find her when they were finished with them here.

Turning her head slightly so she could see the chair next to hers, Elsa suddenly understood what was going to happen to them. Before she could rise from her seat, the vulture standing behind her pushed Elsa's head forward so that her chin rested on her chest. Gripping the arms of the chair, Elsa tried to rise, but the woman slammed her back down and cursed at her. All Elsa could do was listen as the first snipping sound came dangerously close to her ear.

This can't be happening, Elsa thought, as she watched her hair fall into clumps on her lap. Long, gorgeous lengths of hair floated dream-like to the floor until finally all that dropped were short nubs that looked as if they were shaved off. When she was able to lift her hand to her head, all she felt was the nubby softness of hair less than half a centimeter short. It was a haircut much like Josef was wearing.

Josef.

She hoped he wasn't afraid. Maybe he was with all of the other children playing marbles or building things. She so wanted to believe that. Surely the Nazis weren't so barbaric as to harm little children? That was unthinkable. She preferred to think of Josef and her Papa working in the camp bakery or doing some other manual labor.

"*Aus!*" the woman grunted, and Elsa immediately jumped to her feet. There was something particularly disturbing about stepping on the layers of hair on the floor. It felt as if so much more than hair had been cut away from her. Staring down at the hair Marissa found so beautiful, Elsa inhaled very slowly.

Marissa.

Where was she? Why hadn't she answered Elsa when she called her name? Did these guards mean to leave Elsa with no one? Did the Germans wish to strip her of everything? As fear and panic gripped her, Elsa looked around desperately, like a trapped animal searching for a way out.

"Keep moving or she'll hit you again," came a tiny voice from behind her.

Looking over her shoulder, Elsa saw a small, dwarf-like woman wearing the same haircut she envisioned she wore.

"Your friend, the one you kept calling for, is okay. I saw them take her into another building to the left of this one."

Elsa swallowed back her relief. "Thank you." Elsa turned around and tried to look out of the dirty window.

"I am Katya," the small woman whispered. "My friends call me Kat."

Looking back over her shoulder, Elsa tried to smile. Katya was probably close to Elsa's age, with fuzzy blonde nubs and bright blue eyes. Her smile, though gentle, had a wizened look about it. But the most interesting feature about her was her size. She only came up to Elsa's shoulder.

"I am Elsa," she replied, still staring down into Katya's wise face. "Can you tell me why they've done this?"

"What? Caged us or cut off our hair?"

"Both."

"They cut our hair off so we won't get head lice. And we're here to be worked to death. I heard rumors that this is a death camp."

The word seemed to freeze Elsa. "Death camp? You mean for the Jews?"

Katya nodded. "These are just rumors, mind you. Hitler can't possibly be serious about destroying an entire race of people."

Elsa thought back to the rumors Marissa had been sharing with her, and now, here they were, all because she was too stubborn to leave her Papa behind. Perhaps she could have tried harder to convince him. Perhaps she should have just taken Josef and left. Perhaps . . .

As they were roughly ushered into another room, Elsa instinctively grabbed Katya's hand. After having her hair cut, Elsa could not imagine what they would take from her next.

"What room is this?" Elsa whispered before harsh hands pushed her into yet another chair. The German guards were gruffing out orders and grousing with each other, and Elsa had a difficult time following instructions.

Grabbing her left arm, a skinny apparition of a woman slammed it on the table. In her right hand, the woman held some kind of tool. In the next five seconds, Elsa discovered that the tool was used for tattooing.

The pain from the tattooer bolted up her arm and pounded to a stop at her temples. Closing her eyes, Elsa tried to think of something pleasant to ease her mind of the stabbing pain. She remembered when she and Marissa shared their first real kiss.

They had just returned from a long, intense lunch where Marissa's tales of the underground enthralled her. She had never met anyone as strong and as opinionated as Marissa, and she loved to listen to her for hours.

When they returned to the shop, Papa told her that business was slow so she could go upstairs and entertain Marissa. By now, Marissa was part of the family, her Papa having given in long ago to their friendship.

Marissa had no real family. When her parents were killed when she was yet a teenager, she moved in with her aunt and uncle, who wanted nothing more than to marry her off to some wealthy merchant. When Marissa told them that she had a job and wanted to pay for her room and board, they waved both her and her money off and told her to leave their house. She left and rented a small studio from a couple Madame knew well. So whenever she got the chance to be around Elsa and her family, Marissa did so.

Elsa smiled, remembering Marissa plopping down on the bed with her hands behind her head. For the longest time, she silently studied Elsa.

"You are a most beautiful woman," Marissa had said at last.

Elsa blushed. "I did not suspect you to be the flattering sort."

Propping up on her elbow, Marissa grinned. "I'm not. I simply tell the truth."

"Oh?"

"Yes." Marissa hesitated, sitting fully up on the bed and patting the space next to her. "And I have been . . . I need to . . ."

"What is this? Marissa Kowalski is speechless?"

"No. It's just that I do not have the words to tell you I feel for you in a way that . . . might make you uncomfortable."

Elsa sat next to Marissa. Her green eyes were a forest green and reflected the sincerity of her words. "And what way is that?"

Placing her hand on top of Elsa's, Marissa gave it a slight squeeze. "I have never felt this close to anyone in my life, Elsa. At first, I tried to excuse my feelings as some sort of familial need."

"But?"

"But then I realized that it wasn't that at all. I . . . I love you, Elsa. And not like a sister either. I . . . I find myself always wanting to touch your hair or caress your face. Many times when you speak, I become so entranced by the movement of your lips, I do not hear your words."

Elsa smiled slightly. She did not feel the discomfort Marissa had anticipated. Instead, she felt a warm relief that the subject had finally been broached.

"I have often wondered what you found so interesting about my mouth."

Marissa inched nearer. "What I find is that I am always thinking about kissing it, about kissing you. I wish to feel closer to you. I . . . I believe you feel the same for me."

Elsa's face burned red. "I do."

And without thinking about it, without analyzing it any further, she and Marissa leaned into each other's embrace and kissed each other warmly for a long, long time.

"Ouch!" Elsa cried, the sting of the tattooer bringing her back to her bleak reality. Gazing down at her left forearm, Elsa saw the numbers 12575 inked there. Like cattle they were branded, each with their own number and no real identity.

Standing next to Katya as they were thrown their camp clothes, Elsa stared down at the gray and white striped uniforms. It was the final frame of reality fluttering across the screen. They were prisoners now. Prisoners without hair, without possessions, without each other. Standing in the line, Elsa noted how alike they all looked now. Only the tattooed arms distinguished one from another. In less than three hours, the Nazis had managed to erase their identities.

Burying her head in her scratchy bundled uniform, Elsa wept for the last time.

Chapter Ten

"Because Elsa wore the yellow star of a Jew, her life was to be much harder than mine." Marissa grabbed the podium with both hands. "While I was wearing the red triangle of a Pole, it certainly did not guarantee life, but it was not looked upon with the revulsion the yellow star received. It was one of the reasons I was not with Elsa when she was getting her head shaved. I was soon to find out what the other reason was."

Walking into the stuffy barracks, Marissa's olfactory was inundated with sour smells of body odor, urine, sour milk, and heat that blended together to create a stench that was nearly impossible to inhale. There was another burning smell that hung more heavily than the others, but Marissa could not distinguish it.

Wiping her watery eyes, Marissa looked up at the rows and rows of triple-layer bunk beds lining the long walls of the barracks. There were at least two women to each bed; in most cases, the beds held three. But it wasn't the number of women crammed into such a small living space that astounded her. It was the hollow cheeks and haunted eyes of a hundred women staring vacantly at the new arrivals. These women and their tortured gazes were more macabre specters than people. At a glance, they all looked similar, with their striped uniforms, their shaved heads, and that look; the look of the spiritually empty, the defeated; it was the look of a truth Marissa did not think she could ever comprehend.

Stepping over to a bed that had only two women in it, Marissa self-consciously touched her hair. There were others who kept their hair as well, but Marissa noted that none of them wore the blazing star.

"A Pole, eh?"

Marissa searched for the body that the detached voice came from and found it looking down at her with the grayest eyes she had ever seen.

"Don't be shy, lady, or you'll end up sleeping on the floor." The woman with the almost white eyes was wearing her shoulder-length, blonde hair in a ponytail, and it bobbed up and down whenever she spoke.

Marissa only grinned sheepishly and nodded. All eyes in the room seemed to be waiting for her response.

"Oh, don't mind the others. They're always jealous of those of us who get to keep our hair." Gray Eyes sat up and swung her legs over the edge of the bunk.

She was a very striking woman, with a strong jaw and high cheekbones. Her strange eyes aside, there was a strength in her face that Marissa had not seen on any of the others.

Suddenly, a new voice permeated the thick, waiting silence.

"Stefanie, if you do not shut up, one of them will come over here and cut off your whole damned head."

The woman named Stefanie hopped off the bed and offered her hand to Marissa.

"Stefanie Sukova, Czech."

Marissa shook her hand. "Marissa Kowalski."

"Don't mind my grumpy bunkmate. She's a rather pessimistic sort."

Stefanie tightened her ponytail and grinned into Marissa's face. They were nearly the same height.

"Welcome to the Devil's Last Dance."

"Stefanie!" her, as of yet, invisible bunkmate cried.

Lowering her voice, Stefanie whispered to Marissa, "She hates it when I'm glib. Says that God, whoever THAT is, will send me to be gassed."

Marissa's eyes widened. "Gassed?"

Putting her arm around Marissa, Stefanie led her to the window. "You might as well hear the truth about this place now." Stefanie pointed out the window. It was almost dark, and a heavy pallor hung like fog in the sky. "Look outside, M. Tell me what you see."

"Stefanie," her bunkmate hissed. "You could have waited a little longer before heaping that burden on her shoulders."

"That's where you're wrong, C. I think everyone should know what they're up against as soon as they get here." Then to Marissa, "Being ignorant never kept anyone alive in this place. Go on. Tell me what you see."

Marissa stepped up to the window and peered through the dirty panes. The evening sky was an eerie red, and a faint haze seemed to rise out of the forest. In the far distance, she could barely make out a roof with a chimney billowing grayish smoke.

"Welcome to Hitler's *Vernichtungslager*."

Marissa turned from the window with questioning eyes. "Death camp?"

"More like annihilation camp. Sorry to be the one to break it to you, but they brought you here to work you to death. We've all been brought here to die."

"Stefanie Sukova, shut your mouth this instant. Do you hear me?"

Stefanie leaned closer to Marissa. "Most refuse to believe it. Well, I've been here over a year, and I speak fluent German. I've heard those crazy Nazi bastards actually laughing about it. It's insane."

Yes, Marissa thought to herself. It is. Looking back out the window, she shuddered. "What is the smoke from?"

"The ovens. After they gas them, they cremate 'em in the ovens. When the wind changes tonight, you'll smell it. I don't smell anything anymore. The stench ruined my smeller, I think. No great loss. The food's not worth tasting anyway."

Marissa felt her legs weaken at the thought of huge ovens crammed with bodies. Lots of bodies.

"Stefanie, I . . . have a friend—"

"Jew?"

"Yes."

"Woman?"

"Yes."

"Healthy?"

Marissa nodded.

"Where did they send her when you got off the train?"

"Into a large building that—"

"Good. Then she was spared . . . for the moment. They sent her in to have her head shaved like the rest."

Marissa sank against the windowsill. "For the moment" reverberated in her head.

"Were there others in your family?"

Marissa started to shake her head, but then thought of Josef and Mr. Liebowitz. "Yes. Her Papa and little brother."

Stefanie looked out the window and shook her head sadly. Her gray eyes seemed the same color as the smoke as she peered past Marissa's shoulder and into the night.

"Then they have become timber for the flames, I'm afraid."

Marissa gripped the windowsill. "What?"

"Older and younger male Jews are the first to go here. Were they sent down the gravel path?"

Marissa was afraid to nod, afraid to even speak.

Seeing Marissa's distress, Stefanie pulled her away from the window and back to her bunk. "Death is something that you have to get used to now. You mustn't allow it to debilitate you, or you will end up like they did."

Marissa shook her head and tried to stave off the wave of nausea climbing up her throat. "Get used to death? Who could get used to death and still keep their humanity?"

Helping Marissa up the bunk, Stefanie sighed. "Everyone alive in here, that's who. You listen to me, M. All you worry about in here is making sure that you don't become fuel for the fire. That's all you'll have the energy to do, believe me."

Marissa climbed into the bunk as the large woman named C. huffed and rolled on her side. "How long did you say you'd been in here?"

"Somewhere between a year and a lifetime. No one ever really knows. Besides, that doesn't really matter. What matters is that I'm alive when they open those gates."

Marissa tried to keep her eyes open so she could see Elsa when she came through the door, but the day had been long and emotionally painful, and she could not will them to stay open any longer.

"Hey, M.," came Stefanie's voice from far away. "What's your friend's name, so I can be on the lookout for her?"

"Elsa. Elsa Liebowitz."

Chapter Eleven

When the door to the barracks clattered open, Marissa rose quickly and bumped her head. Jumping off the bed, she was surprised to see Stefanie waiting for her.

"What are you doing?" Marissa asked, watching the line of tired, bedraggled women filing in.

"I like to know who I'm living with, that's all. Call me curious."

"Call her nosy," came C.'s voice from above.

As the line of frightened women huddled past, Marissa frantically searched every shaved head until she finally came to the last woman.

"She's not here!" Gripping Stefanie's arm, she repeated her cry.

"Hold on, M., she may have just been assigned to a different barracks. Is she a seamstress too?"

Marissa stopped breathing and tilted her head at Stefanie as if she didn't understand the question.

"What?"

"You're in here to sew for the almighty Reich. You DO know how to sew, don't you?"

Marissa still did not answer.

"Oh, for crying out loud, M., don't stand there like a dumb Pollock, say something."

Marissa looked out at the chimneys beckoning, tormenting her. "Sew? I have to sew?"

"No, M., you GET to sew. That's why I've stayed alive so damned long in this hell hole. All of us in here sew. We work in the warehouse across the path."

Marissa turned back and nodded. Suddenly, it made sense. She remembered the plaque in the front about work making you free. "I understand. Yes, I do sew."

Stefanie clapped her hands together. "Good! And Elsa, does she sew as well?"

Marissa shook her head. "A baker's daughter."

Stefanie frowned. "Well, all is not lost. She's been put in the work detail. In the morning, we'll take a look through the compound and see if we can't find out what work detail she is on. If that doesn't work, I have a few connections."

"How did they know?"

Stefanie shrugged. "Your papers. The Nazis go through every paper to see who is of value to the Reich. It's your lucky day. Today, they need seamstresses."

"Stefanie Sukova, do I have to come down there and shut you up myself?"

Stefanie grinned at Marissa. "Claudia thinks she's the reason I've lasted so long."

"Is she?"

"Hell no. I just take good care of myself, if you know what I mean."

Marissa didn't, but let it go.

"Tomorrow, they'll have another selection for the new men they brought in. That will be when we look."

"Selection?"

"That's when they decide who lives and who dies. Kind of like the Romans used to do to gladiators. If you're too weak or sick to work, they'll select you for *Sonderbehandlung*. That's German for special handling of undesirables. C. always mispronounces it. But make no mistake; no matter how you say it, the word means death."

"But what of those signs that say work will make you free?"

"Don't you believe it. No one escapes from Auschwitz, and no one is ever set free. The damned signs should read: Work to live, don't and die. Rather catchy, don't you think?"

By now, Marissa didn't know what to think. So many nightmares seemed to come to life at once. She had heard such stories from her friends in the Resistance, but she couldn't imagine . . . surely no one could believe that this was actually happening?

"Come now, M., you should get some sleep. I'm sure your journey has been an exhausting one."

The word exhausting seemed to hit an energy switch in Marissa, and she suddenly felt unable to hold herself up. "I suppose you're right."

"Of course I am. I'm an old hand at this by now. You'll see."

Laying down on the bunk, Marissa tried not to hear the sounds of men and women screaming or the popping of guns being shot through the night. She tried to ignore the flash of light that swept past the window every twelve seconds. She covered her ears from the wheezing sounds of women sleeping and panting, grunting sounds of those who were not.

But most of all, she tried not to think of the fate that had fallen on Elsa's family in the furnaces not one-hundred meters from where she lay.

Chapter Twelve

It seemed a mere minute since she closed her eyes to the sounds of the night, when she was being dragged to her feet by Stefanie and another woman.

"Get up, M.," Stefanie ordered, pulling her to the floor.

"What? What is it?" For a moment, Marissa did not remember where she was.

"Just stand at attention next to our bunk with your left arm showing."

Marissa did as she was told. Soon, one of the hefty guards entered the room with an assistant carrying a clipboard. She addressed one short, beefy woman wearing the same armband she had seen on the other women who had scooped up their clothes.

"Your productivity is low," the guard announced, slapping a short, black whip in the palm of her black-leathered hand. "Reichsfuhrer SS Himmler demands you pick up the pace. See to it that you double productivity this week, or you and your pathetic bunch of seamstresses will be replaced by someone who can get it done. Do you understand?"

The large-boned woman with the armband nodded. "Yes, Logiernfuhren, I do. I will see to it that your wishes are complied with."

The guard studied her for a moment, and the scene reminded Marissa of two people leaning over a chess set. The large inmate was uncommonly ugly. Her hair was cut short, cropped closely around the ears like a man's haircut would be. Her eyes were too narrow, and her big horse teeth looked as if they should have been in someone else's head. The most remarkable feature about this woman was her hands. She had the largest hands Marissa had ever seen.

"Then do it. I believe you received others to replace those Jews we took yesterday?"

The woman nodded. "We have."

"Then, Fritzi, there shall be no excuses." Turning on her heels, the guard stepped crisply out the door.

No sooner had the door closed than the woman called Fritzi turned and glared at the others.

"How many times must I tell you? Are you all so stupid that you want to die? Every day, I tell you to work faster, and what do you do? Nothing! Would you rather be out digging trenches in this heat with all the others?" Her square jaw now jutted out with obvious authority. "From now on, no breaks. You will work until you have doubled the day's quota."

Marissa saw movement out of the corner of her eye and realized it was Stefanie.

"Working us to death won't double our quota, Fritzi, and you know it."

Marissa stared straight ahead as Fritzi walked past her. Fritzi's anger rushed by in a heated wind.

"What I know, Sukova, is that you and your people will do it or be replaced."

For a second, Marissa thought Fritzi was going to hit Stefanie.

"First of all, it is impossible to sew with thread-like fishing line. Secondly, you know damn well that we've been four women short for some time now. Give it a rest."

"Always the advocate, eh, Sukova? You know where that gets you."

Stefanie shrugged. "Take away our breaks, and we'll make sure we don't fill your damned quota. Where will that get you, oh mighty Kapo?"

The two women glared harshly at each other with neither giving ground. All eyes stared at the pair of statues as they stood silently weighing each other.

And then, to Marissa's surprise, Fritzi walked away. "You may keep your insignificant breaks as long as you double the quota. But mind me, Stefanie Sukova, once you fail, you will work through the night if you have to in order to finish the job." With that, Fritzi slammed out the door, leaving a commotion in her wake.

Marissa did not know what to say when Stefanie turned to her and grinned.

"Scare you?"

Marissa nodded.

"You have really angered her now, Stef," Claudia grumbled, rolling her sleeve back down.

"She was bluffing. She needs us."

"She'll come after you if you're not more careful. Look at what she did to Anna, Bettye and Gerta."

Stefanie waved her off. "They were Jews caught stealing. They should have been more careful than that."

"Still—"

Stefanie turned and ran her hand playfully over the woman's nubby hair. "You worry too much, my grumpy friend."

"And you take many chances."

Stefanie laughed. "Chances are all there is to take here. What will playing it safe get you? Come on, C., we have work to do. We have to help M. find her friend."

The entire time, Marissa had stood motionless at her bunk. The politics of Auschwitz was something altogether new and different, and Marissa wasn't sure she quite understood the pecking order.

Looking at Claudia for the first time, Marissa tried to grin. "I'm Marissa."

"I'm Claudia," the large woman replied. Her broad shoulders and keen eyes reminded Marissa of a watch dog, always ready to pounce. "Stefanie calls me C. Too lazy for full names, I guess." She turned and winked at Stefanie, who was still grinning.

"Claudia and I met on the train over. Ugh, what a horrible ride that was. She lost her mother, two sisters, and their three children, so you'll have to excuse her if she's a bit on the grouchy side."

Claudia shook her head. "And you'll have to pardon Stef's insanity. She doesn't believe in following the rules even in a death camp."

"Who was that woman with the armband?" Marissa asked.

"Her? She's the Kapo. Short for *Kammeradschafts Polizei.*"

Marissa's eyebrows rose. "Friendly police?" The label was absurd.

Stefanie nodded. "Close enough. The Nazis don't have enough manpower to run this damned place, so they put us in charge of each other. Pretty bizarre, don't you think?"

Marissa nodded. "You mean there are more like her?"

"Unfortunately. And believe me when I say they are all cut from the same ugly cloth. They're mean and cruel and believe themselves to be better than we are."

"Why?"

"Because they get special treatment for their cruelty. Fritzi's in charge of the warehouse. Her job is to make sure we work until we drop. When we perform well, she is the only one rewarded."

Marissa felt a tremor of fear run along her spine.

"But don't worry. She doesn't mess with me or my friends."

For the first time, Marissa realized there was an elaborate hierarchy, and she was a small part of it. "And my friend?"

"We'll take a look on the compound this morning on our way to the warehouse. If she survived the night, she should be there."

"Stefanie!" Claudia admonished.

Stefanie smirked at Marissa and shrugged. "The truth now or the truth later will always be the truth. Might as well get used to it. Death is always right outside the back door. I think it's better to acknowledge it's there than to ignore it."

"Couldn't you at least give her some time?"

"Time, my friend, is something none of us has."

Following Claudia and Stefanie to the door, Marissa felt her heart banging inside her chest. For the first time, the impact of what was going on around her hit her with full force. And as she stepped into the harsh glare of the sun, Marissa did something she hadn't done since she was a child.

She prayed.

Chapter Thirteen

The compound was a hectic, bustling swarm of chaos as inmates were herded from one place to another. Looking out over the sea of shaved heads and gray and white striped jackets, Marissa began to wonder whether or not she would even be able to pick Elsa out among the throngs of prisoners.

"Just keep following Fritzi, M., and look for your friend. When we get to the next set of barracks, C. and I will create a small diversion."

Marissa nodded and started walking in shoes that were too small for her feet. Her eyes burned from the night stench of the furnaces, and her back ached from sleeping on the hard bunk.

Just as they reached the next set of barracks, Marissa heard Elsa's voice.

"Mari!"

Instantly, Marissa turned and saw Elsa's shaved head pushing through the crowd.

"Mari!"

As Marissa stepped toward her, Claudia and Stefanie each grabbed an arm and moved her away from Elsa.

"Let me go!" Marissa warned, struggling to break free.

"Stop it! You mustn't break rank, M.," Stefanie shouted, pulling Marissa along.

Head still turned, eyes locked on the woman she loved, Marissa painfully understood why Claudia and Stefanie had stopped her.

Just as Elsa had pushed her way through the crowd, the black arm of a guard struck her to the ground, and his long black boot kicked her in the stomach.

"No!" Marissa cried, struggling against their vice-grips. "Elsa!" Watching helplessly as the guards kicked Elsa again, Marissa ceased fighting and turned her face away. She could not bear to see Elsa treated so inhumanely.

"Come on, M.," Stefanie said, reaching her arm around Marissa and drawing her to her side. "There is nothing you can do for her."

"Elsa," Marissa muttered, stopping to take another look. Two women, one who was no taller than Josef, bent over and picked Elsa up.

"I . . . love you, Mari," Elsa's noiseless lips said.

Marissa's only response was a nod as she pressed her fingers to her mouth.

"Unless you want to be treated to the same punishment as your friend, M., you must come inside."

Claudia nodded and urged her forward. "Don't get Fritzi angry with you on your first day, Marissa. Come inside."

Marissa gazed over her shoulder one final time before stepping into the warehouse. She had never felt so far away from Elsa as she did at this moment.

"There is a bright side to this, M. At least you know she's alive."

"But not if she tries that again," Claudia said, shaking her head.

Slowly turning away, Marissa stared beyond the massive barbed wire fence and into the fringe of the surrounding trees. It seemed impossible that there was a world out there that went to the store and bought bread or walked down the street with a child. Two days ago, she was a part of that world. Now . . . now she was walking in someone else's nightmare.

"Stef?"

"Yes?"

"I want you to teach me how to survive this place."

Stefanie threaded her arm through Marissa's as they walked to their sewing machines. "M., there's only one thing you need to know, and that is always look out for number one. Take care of yourself first. Don't spend your energy worrying about anything else except yourself. Do that, and you'll live. Start caring too much about others, and it will destroy you. Right, C.?"

Claudia only half nodded. "Something like that."

Sitting at her machine, Marissa stared out the one window. What was this horror she was caught in, and how could she get out?

Chapter Fourteen

Elsa suddenly joined Marissa at the podium. "What Mari could not have known at the time was just how close I came to being shot. Prisoners in Auschwitz never run unless they are running away. Had not Stefanie and Claudia stopped her, they might have killed the both of us.

"But to know Marissa was alive was worth the beating the guard gave me. It was most eerie the way the physical pain overshadowed my tormented spirit. It was much easier dealing with the corporeal wounds that the deep emotional scars inflicted when she and my family were taken from me. So often, others died more from the emotional losses than the physical pain."

"How much further must we go?" Elsa heard an older woman ask.

"Quiet."

Elsa and Katya walked in silence for some time before speaking.

"Mari is a beautiful woman," Katya offered at last.

Elsa nodded. "Yes, she is."

"I've been listening to the Hungarian women behind us. They think that one of their friends was taken to the warehouse where your friend is."

Elsa turned and waited.

"They say that the woman is a seamstress and is being housed with others who work in the warehouse. Is Mari a seamstress?"

"Yes. Yes, she is."

"Then that is why you were separated. She has a particular skill the Nazis can make use of. We, well . . . we're just manual laborers at this point."

Elsa nodded, looking down at her soft hands. The only manual labor she ever did was pound on bread dough; hardly what she would call physical work or a particular skill.

"Katya, how is it you speak Hungarian?"

"My mother is a Hungarian Jew. I last saw her when they liquidated our ghetto."

"Then you are alone here?"

Katya shrugged and wiped sweat off her forehead. "I am now. I have three brothers, but I do not know where they have been sent."

Still looking at Katya, Elsa stumbled and grabbed her ribs that ached from the steely kicks of the guards.

"Are you okay?"

Lightly fingering her ribs, Elsa nodded. "Sore, but I'll live. That wasn't very smart of me to go off running like that."

"Stupid is the word I would use," came a voice from behind them.

Elsa and Kat both turned to find a woman almost six-feet tall wearing a red bandanna wrapped around her head. Elsa immediately spied the yellow armband on her arm.

"Acting like that will get you killed next time, or worse."

"Or worse?"

The giant nodded. "Doktor Mengele is worse than death, worse than the devil. There are crueller fates in life than death, my ignorant little Jews, and one of them is being sent to him. Remember that, next time you try to run off to visit with one of your friends."

Katya turned away, disgusted with the sharp, condescending tone of this woman. Elsa, however, did not.

"Have you been here long?"

The woman grinned. Her teeth were slightly yellow, and there was a chip off one of her front teeth. "Long enough to know that you're going to have to be smarter than that if you're going to survive."

Katya grabbed Elsa and turned her around. "Don't listen to her, Elsa. She is just trying to frighten us."

Suddenly, the large woman took one stride and was walking next to them. "I hope it's working because there is a great deal more to be afraid of here."

"Such as?"

"Such as never seeing those you love alive again."

This struck a chord so loud it resounded through Elsa's whole being.

"My name is Yvonne, and I am the Kapo of our unit. I can help you see your friend, if that is what you wish."

Elsa stopped walking, but Katya urged her on. "You can? How? When?"

Katya frowned at Elsa, but she pretended not to see it.

"I have connections, but it will cost you. No one does anything in Auschwitz for free."

"I have nothing."

Yvonne smiled, her yellow teeth barely touching her lips. "Oh, everyone has something to give."

"I'd give anything."

"No!" Katya cried, grabbing Elsa's arm. "Her price will be much too high. I've heard how these Kapos work. They are the worst prisoners here. Like leeches, they will suck you dry and then cast you aside. Don't let her tempt you."

"I must, Kat." Turning to Yvonne, Elsa nodded. "What is it you require for this . . . favor?"

Yvonne was still grinning. "You'll see. It will not be a price beyond your capabilities to pay. What is her name?"

"Marissa. Marissa Kowalski."

"I'll see what I can do. In the meantime, try to avoid drawing attention to yourself. It could cost you your life."

Elsa nodded.

"And you, little one," Yvonne said, addressing Katya, "should not be so suspicious. I may wear this armband, but not all of us are monsters." And as quickly as she came, Yvonne disappeared into the crowd trudging behind them.

"Elsa, you don't know what you're doing. Who knows what she has in mind for payment. Didn't you . . ." Katya lowered her voice. "Didn't you hear some of those noises last night? You know as well as I do what they were."

Elsa stared straight ahead. "Perhaps, but I do not believe that is what she will want from me."

"Suppose she does? What will you do then?" Katya's voice was a pitch higher than usual.

"Then I will have to make other arrangements, that's all. Really, Katya, it cannot be as bad as all that."

"Well, I hope not, Elsa, for your sake."

Chapter Fifteen

Five days went by before Yvonne approached Elsa again.

"Your friend is making quite a stir in the warehouse," Yvonne said, plopping down on the edge of Elsa's bunk. "They say she's so good she alone has helped them reach their quota. Not bad."

Elsa licked her parched and cracked lips and waited for more. The last five days had been an education in survival for Elsa and Katya. The second morning, they were awakened by loud noises, and Elsa looked up in time to see half a dozen women hovering over a bunk. When the crowd dispersed, Elsa looked down in horror at the graying body laying naked on the bunk.

"What's happening?" she asked Katya, who had been sitting up watching.

"She's dead. They stole her clothes."

"Off a corpse?"

Katya nodded, rolling away from the scene to face Elsa. "They say it happens all the time. The winters are brutal here. No heat, no blankets, nothing. So everyone loads up getting ready for the winter. Pretty smart if you ask me."

"Katya!"

Suddenly, Kat turned on her. "Look, Elsa, it's kill or be killed, or haven't you noticed? These women act like animals because they've been treated like them for so long; they don't know what humanity means anymore."

Elsa sat up and looked at Katya in the morning light. She looked tinier than she usually did, and her face was almost white. As two large drops rolled down her cheeks, Katya buried her face in her hands.

"But we don't have to become like that, Katya." Taking Katya in her arms, Elsa held her while she sobbed.

"Oh, Elsa, I'm so afraid that will happen to me."

Steadily rocking back and forth, Elsa caressed Katya's blonde nubs. "I won't let that happen to either of us, my little friend."

Katya looked up, eyes red and cheeks burned from too many hours in the sun.

"Promise? Promise me you won't let me act like some vulture preying on the dead."

Cradling her gently in her arms, Elsa kissed the top of her head.

"I promise."

The next day, Elsa saw, first hand, what roll Yvonne played in this macabre scene from some gruesome horror story. When they went out to work, Yvonne ruled with little compassion and a great deal of force. She would rant and rave, hit, kick, and threaten to keep the exhausted women working.

"She is as brutal as the guards," Katya whispered one day.

Elsa shook her head. "She's not so bad."

"How can you say that when you've seen what she's capable of doing? She looks like she enjoys the brutality."

"What is the alternative to work, Katya?"

"Death."

"Or worse?"

Katya nodded. "Or worse."

"Then she keeps us alive by making us work."

"Only to line her own pockets."

"Does that really matter? Does what anybody does in here really matter as long as we survive?"

"She needn't be so cruel."

"No? Do you think sweet talk will make the weary work?"

"No."

"Then don't be too harsh on her. I should hope that if I ever gave up she would hurt me enough to make me go back to work so that I could go back to living. If she does that to people, she cannot be all bad."

Katya shook her head and touched Elsa's cheek with the back of her hand. "How could I have worried about becoming an animal when I have such a friend? Sometimes, Elsa, you should try seeing the darker side of things."

"Believe me, Kat, I do. But there is a light side to Yvonne. You just have to be willing to see it."

Still shaking her head, Katya sighed. "We'll see."

And now, with Yvonne perched on the side of her bunk, it was time to do just that.

"Apparently, Marissa Kowalski is quite adept at sewing and has shown the others some new techniques. The Logiernfuhren is quite pleased."

Elsa folded her arms and waited. She did not care what price Yvonne was extracting, she would pay just to have Marissa in her arms for a single moment.

"As a result, the women have been given better quality things to work with; you know, thread, material, needles, that kind of thing. That material is to be delivered by myself, their Kapo, and two other workers."

Elsa studied Yvonne's sharp nose and square jawline. She was not a beautiful woman, but she wasn't ugly either. There was something about her blue eyes that told Elsa there was much more to this woman than what she displayed.

"When?"

"Tomorrow morning. I will come get you, and we will deliver the supplies. One word of caution: if you act like you did the other day, you'll have more to worry about than just a few kicks. Understand?"

Elsa nodded. "Yes. Thank you, Yvonne." Elsa turned to leave, but Yvonne's hand was heavy on her wrist, pulling her back.

"My payment?"

Feeling the heat of the room double in intensity, Elsa exhaled slowly. "And that is?"

"Your little friend, Katya."

Yanking her wrist away, Elsa stood up. "What about her?"

Yvonne frowned and lowered her voice. "I would wish for her to know . . . to know . . . that I . . . find her attractive."

59

Elsa cocked her head. "Excuse me?"

"I simply want her to know that she does not have to spend her nights alone if she chooses not to. I . . . I would like to be with her."

Pinching the bridge of her nose, Elsa thought she had just about heard it all. "And all you want is for me to tell her this?"

"Yes. And if anyone else hears about this, you'll have said your last words." Standing up, Elsa could see that Yvonne's cheeks were flushed.

"But suppose . . . suppose she doesn't feel . . ."

"That's no matter," Yvonne replied almost angrily. "I just want her to know."

"Then why don't you tell her yourself?"

"No. I do not think she fully understands my position here. Coming from me, it would sound like a threat. I do not want to frighten her. I do not want her to feel like she must come to me. I would wish she choose to on her own accord."

Nodding as if she understood, Elsa stepped aside and let Yvonne pass.

"Yvonne, why me? Is it because we are friends?"

Yvonne nodded. "That, and I saw the look in your eyes when you went after Kowalski. Whenever you speak of her, I sense there is . . . more. I . . . had a friend like that once. She was gassed the hour after we arrived."

Watching Yvonne walk away, Elsa could only shake her head. Nothing that happened at Auschwitz could surprise her now.

Absolutely nothing.

Chapter Sixteen

"Well?" Katya asked, climbing into the bunk after what had been their hardest workday. Elsa had not told her yet; too many ears to hear, and she did not doubt that Yvonne meant what she had said.

"Tomorrow morning."

Katya laid on her stomach and leaned on her elbows. "And what's her price?"

Swallowing back her trepidation, Elsa looked hard at Kat. The lack of food and harsh work was already taking its toll on her tiny body. Her eyes had that same, empty gaze as the others, and her cheeks were becoming hollow and pale. The sun had burned her scalp, making her whole head peel. She was not looking nearly as healthy as when they arrived, and Elsa briefly wondered what she, herself, must look like.

"Elsa, you're stalling."

"Yes . . . yes, I am."

Katya's blue eyes haunted Elsa now as she waited for an answer.

"Tell me."

Wiping her mouth, Elsa inhaled slowly. "She . . . Yvonne wants me to . . . "

"To what?"

"To tell you . . . that she . . . is attracted to you."

Katya's eyes grew large. "What?"

"She said—"

"I heard what you said. But what does she mean? I mean, what could she want?"

Elsa reached out and patted Katya's hand. "I don't think she wants anything other than for you to know that. What you do with that information is up to you."

"Up to me? Does she honestly think—"

"Katya." Elsa held up a hand to silence her. "The woman obviously finds you interesting and beautiful. She did not say that she wanted to take you to bed."

61

"Well it's implied, isn't it?"

"Is it?" Elsa's eyebrows raised in question.

"I . . . I don't know. I don't know what to say."

"You do not have to say anything."

"You're holding something back, aren't you?" Katya leaned closer to Elsa.

"That is all she said. I swear."

For a moment, Katya and Elsa stared at each other with neither saying a word. All around them, women tossed and turned in sweat-covered dreams, while outside people's screams and misery were heard over the barking dogs and gun shots ringing through the night air.

Suddenly, Katya put her hand over her mouth and stifled a giggle.

"Why are you laughing?"

"Because all day long, all she did was stare at me. I got so uncomfortable I asked her if I was doing something wrong. And do you know what she said? She said if I was doing something wrong, she'd be more than happy to show me the right way."

"She didn't." Elsa covered her mouth with both hands.

"She did."

"What did you say?"

"What could I say? I didn't understand, so I just walked away."

Elsa touched Katya's earlobe; the only place she wasn't sunburnt. "She's not an awful person, you know. I think it's kind of . . . cute that she likes you so much."

Katya grinned shyly and turned her head away. "It might be cute if she wasn't the law in here. Scary is more like it. What should I do?"

"Nothing. If you're not interested, I don't think she will bother you. But if she comes to you, you better know what your decision is and what you want to say to her."

Katya nodded. "Elsa, do you think the women who do that sort of thing here did it when they were free?"

Thoughts of Marissa floated through Elsa's mind. "I would imagine."

"Do you think," Katya said, lowering her voice. "Do you think she would force me?"

Elsa shook her head. "No, I don't think sex is the only thing Yvonne is looking for, Kat."

"What else is there?"

Elsa smiled and put her arm around Katya's tiny shoulders. "Love."

"Don't be silly, Elsa. There's no love in this place; there's only animal behaviors like eating, sleeping, going to the bathroom, and being herded from one place to another."

"You are wrong, Katya. Love and hope are the two emotions that will keep us alive. Don't sound so bitter, my little friend. I will not let you become so negative."

Katya grinned. "And I won't let you be such an optimist."

Hugging Katya before going to relieve herself, Elsa wondered what Marissa was doing. What was she thinking about all of this? Did she lay awake at night and wonder if Elsa was thinking about her? Was Marissa, as Elsa was doing, hinging her survival on the strength of their love?

Closing her eyes and feeling the intensity of that love, Elsa was convinced she would prove Katya wrong.

Chapter Seventeen

"Reichsfuhrer Himmler is pleased with your production and output, and since he is, he graciously honors Kowalski's request for better supplies." Fritzi grinned a smile which was menacing even when she was laughing. "But this does not mean you are to let down. As always, you will work until the quota has been met."

Stefanie and Claudia exchanged glances that did not go unnoticed by the Kapo. "Is there a comment you would like to add, Sukova?"

Stefanie shook her head. "No. It's just that we've doubled our production, and you never brought us the extra milk you promised."

Fritzi took a step toward Stefanie, and Marissa stared down at the large hands forming fists. She might have hit Stefanie if the door hadn't banged open and Logiernfuhren Werner strode in.

"You are to be congratulated for your speed and productivity, Fritzi," she remarked when everyone had snapped to attention. "You manage these girls well."

Fritzi gave the single nod response Marissa had seen so many Nazis give to each other. It was odd how Fritzi managed to cross the line between ally and enemy; such a precarious balance, such a thin line in the camp. What Marissa hated the most was the way Fritzi stared at the other women whenever they were naked. It chilled her to think of the large-boned woman drooling over the emaciated inmates. There was something strangely obscene about Fritzi's treatment of her fellow prisoners, but Marissa wasn't sure what it was.

"One of the SS wives found this before it was delivered to the German Welfare Office." Werner turned to her assistant and pulled something out of a bag. At once, Marissa knew what it was; it was the dress Elsa wore the day they came to camp; the dress Marissa had made for her. "She wishes to know if one of you can reproduce it."

Marissa licked her lips and looked around at the other seamstresses. A few were nodding their heads, but there was one set of eyes practically drilling a hole through Marissa. They were the chilling gray eyes of Stefanie Sukova.

"I can," Marissa offered. "I can reproduce that dress exactly, Logiernfuhren Werner."

Werner stepped up to Marissa and glared hard at her. Marissa could smell the faint smell of garlic on her breath and some kind of musky-smelling cologne.

"Is that so?"

"She's lying," Fritzi suddenly blurted out.

Whirling around, Werner stared at Fritzi, who was turning a deep shade of red.

"What I mean to say, Logiernfuhren Werner, is that Kowalski is trying to find an easier job. I don't believe she is capable of doing work of that quality."

"Oh, pipe down, Fritz-brain. You're just afraid of losing Marissa because she has the fastest pair of hands of us all." This came from Stefanie, who glowered at Fritzi with contempt.

"Silence, all of you!" Wheeling back around, Werner's eyes narrowed. "Is this true? Are you trying to escape hard work?"

"No. That is not true. If you would like, I would be willing to show you just what I can do."

"Oh, you'll prove it alright. And if you are lying, you will have sewn your last piece of cloth."

Marissa nodded, but said nothing. All she could do was look back at the gray eyes riveted to her.

"Your supplies will be delivered this morning. When they arrive, I will expect you to start immediately and to have that dress to me before tomorrow morning. Is that understood?"

Marissa nodded.

As Werner walked out the door, Fritzi flew at Marissa. "How dare you make me look like a fool in front of Werner!" she demanded, grabbing Marissa's sleeve.

Stefanie reached out and pried Fritzi's fingers loose. "You need no help in that endeavor, I'm afraid."

Before Stefanie could move, Fritzi raised her other hand and quickly backhanded Stefanie's face, sending her crashing to the floor. In an instant, Claudia was at Stefanie's side.

"Let go of me, Fritzi," Marissa threatened.

"Or what?"

Marissa saw light facial hair covering Fritzi's chin and long nose hairs poking out. "Or I'll make you."

Raising her fist to strike Marissa, Fritzi snarled. "You and who else?"

But before she could bring the fist crashing down on her, Marissa saw Claudia's hand grab Fritzi's while it was cocked in the air and quickly twisted it behind Fritzi's back. The grimace on Fritzi's face revealed the pain from her contorted limb.

"Don't make me have to break your arm, Fritzi," Claudia growled, twisting her arm for emphasis. "You wouldn't be of any use to the guards with a broken arm, now would you?"

Marissa stared at the two women locked together. It was inconceivable to her how they couldn't possibly be on the same side. The world had gone crazy and taken all of them with it.

Suddenly, Stefanie appeared in front of them. "What'll it be Fritzi? You going to apologize, or are you going to force me to have C. snap your arm?"

"You wouldn't." It was clearly Fritzi's last attempt to save face.

Claudia put a little more torque on the elbow. "I have nothing to lose by snapping it in two, Fritzi. Just give me a reason."

"Alright! Don't break my arm, for God's sake. I'm sorry I hit Sukova and grabbed Kowalski. Now let me go!"

Shoving Fritzi away, Claudia joined Marissa and Stefanie.

"You've made a big mistake this time, Sukova," Fritzi said, rubbing her arm and shoulder. "We're not finished with this yet." Walking briskly out the door, Fritzi let it slam as it closed.

"Are you okay?" Marissa asked Stefanie, seeing the swelling of her left cheek.

"I'm fine. Thank you, C. That is a nice little move you have there."

Claudia just smiled.

Marissa put her arms around them both. "Thank you both. But aren't we in just a little bit of trouble here?"

Stefanie waved her off. "Forget it."

"I'd like to. I can't help but wonder what you must have on her to be able to talk to her like that."

Stefanie grinned. "Never you mind. Just tell me—can you really get that dress done before morning? I mean, did you get a good look at it? All those darts and button-holes will take some time."

Marissa brushed some dirt off Stefanie's shoulder. "It was my dress to begin with."

Stefanie and Claudia stared at each other. "What?"

"It is my own design," Marissa whispered, moving away from the others. "I gave it to Elsa as a present."

"Why didn't you just say so?" Claudia asked.

"Do you think she would have believed me?"

All three shook their heads.

"I think it's best that we wait to show our hand, and hopefully we can gain something for it."

Stefanie looked perplexed. "And what hand is that?"

Marissa smiled. For the first time, she felt she understood how people stayed alive in these camps.

"You'll see, my little gray-eyed friend. You'll see."

Chapter Eighteen

It was an eternity waiting for the new supplies to arrive. It was the first time Marissa had seen the women excited about something. Better supplies meant they might not have to work so hard or so long to meet their quota. In Auschwitz, she discovered, little victories were celebrated as miracles.

"They're coming!" came the voice from the workers at the window. "And they have boxes and boxes of things!"

Marissa didn't look up from her sewing machine until the doors opened. At first, a very tall Kapo stepped in and whispered something to Fritzi. When Fritzi turned and glared at her, Marissa shifted her gaze back to the work at the machine.

"Kowalski!" Fritzi yelled. "Come here."

Rising from her chair, Marissa looked at Stefanie, who merely shrugged.

"I want you to check everything in," Fritzi said as the other Kapo stood nodding. "You have five minutes, and then I want you back at your machine."

Marissa nodded and glanced over to Stefanie, who wore a perplexed expression. When the taller Kapo with the yellowing teeth opened the door and the bright sunlight streamed in, Marissa squinted at the lithe figure in the doorway.

"Take the box from her, you idiot, and open it." With that, both Kapos went outside.

Still blinded by the sun, Marissa took the box from the woman still standing in the doorway. But as the door closed, Marissa stared at the skinny apparition before her.

"Elsa?" Throwing the box to the floor, Marissa wrapped her arms around her and hugged her tightly. "Is it really you?" Stepping back, Marissa held Elsa's face in her hands. "It is."

Elsa nodded. "I had to see you, my love," Elsa said, laying her hand on Marissa's.

Taking her other hand and touching Elsa's nubs, Marissa's eyes watered.

"It will grow back, Mari. It's only hair."

"Sweetness," Marissa said, backing away and holding Elsa's rough, calloused hands.

"Are you alright? You're so skinny."

"Am I?" Elsa blushed and self-consciously touched her nubby ends. "You look wonderful, Mari. You must be taking good care of yourself."

Marissa shrugged and touched Elsa's sunburned cheek. "Only thoughts of seeing you again push me through every moment. To see you now, to touch you, is better than I ever dreamt. And I dream it often."

Elsa took Marissa's hand from her cheek and held it between her hardened hands. "I had to come; to see you, to feel you. There's so much I need to say before we are separated again."

Marissa squeezed her hand. "I tried to reach you, but my friends—"

"They did what was best. But I am here now, my darling, and that is all that matters."

Marissa looked deep into Elsa's thin face and wide brown eyes. Gone was her wild-deer gaze of an innocent girl. Gone was the naive, dependent young woman who looked to her for support. In such a short time, Elsa transformed into a stronger woman unwilling to accept defeat. In her eyes was a woman so incredibly self-possessed that she held her head higher than she had before they were deported.

"Mari, my love," Elsa said, sitting on the floor and pulling Marissa down next to her. "You are my family now. You are all I have."

"But your Papa and Josef?"

Elsa bowed her head. "Probably dead. You have, no doubt, heard about the killing of Jews. I am afraid that Papa and my Josef were taken to the showers as soon as we arrived."

Marissa took Elsa in her arms, but Elsa gently pushed her away. "I will mourn for them someday, but I have learned some very important points of survival, and one of them is not to worry about those things you have no control over."

"But Elsa—"

"No, Mari, listen. I love you. Knowing that you are still safe and alive keeps me living every day. I need you to promise me that no matter what the cost, you will stay alive."

Marissa brought Elsa's hand to her cheek. "I'll do everything I can, Sweetness, to ensure that we are together when the war is over."

"Promise me."

"I promise."

Elsa smiled gently into Marissa's face. "You are a survivor, Marissa Kowalski. No mater what happens, you must know that I stay alive for the day when we can be together again."

Marissa nodded. "What if one of us should be taken from here? What then?"

"We will meet at Tory's on Tuesday, if it is still there. If it isn't, I will sit on the very spot it used to be and wait an eternity if I have to."

"You won't have to. Not if I can help it."

For a penetrating moment, the two women held hands and looked into each other's changing faces as if to memorize the new version. Both were easily fifteen pounds lighter, and Elsa carried the sun on her face like a mask. Looking down at Elsa's black fingernails, Marissa watched as a teardrop fell onto her hand.

"Don't cry for me, Marissa. No one cries in Auschwitz and lives. Don't you see how lucky we still are? We have each other. We have someone to live for. So many others have nothing."

"I love you, Elsa," Marissa said, holding her frail body in her arms.

"And I, you." Elsa pulled away just as the door reopened. "As long as there's love, Mari, there is hope. Don't ever forget that."

70

"Time's up," came Fritzi's voice as she swaggered into the warehouse.

As the taller Kapo pulled Elsa out the door, Marissa felt her legs tremble. There was a heaviness about the reality surrounding her now that she hadn't noticed before. They really were all alone, and they were fighting just to stay alive for the day they could be reunited. Somehow, before seeing Elsa, it seemed so unreal, so nightmarish. It was as if she would soon snap out of it and come back to reality. Now, reality slapped her hard across the face, and she stood there feeling stunned and afraid. Suddenly, she felt two hands on her shoulders.

"Come on, M., before you make Fritzi mad."

Marissa turned to Stefanie and laughed. "Make her mad? My God, Stef, she is mad. We are all mad. The whole world has gone mad, and we don't even know it."

Stefanie smiled as she sat Marissa down in her chair. "Maybe, but the secret is to accept this new insanity and find a way to live within it."

"Within it?" Suddenly, Marissa felt very old, very tired, and very, very afraid.

Chapter Nineteen

Elsa gripped the podium and inhaled deeply. "Mari says she realized the young girl's innocence was replaced by a more independent woman. The change that Marissa saw in me did not happen all at once. On an hourly basis, we faced atrocities the likes of which this world has never seen. Men and women, tired of being beaten, would hurl themselves into the electric fences to commit suicide. I saw more physical abuse in one day than I had my entire life. Dead bodies were stacked five-feet high, and the only visible difference between the living and the dead was that we wore clothes. But the real change occurred on the day that I learned of Papa and Josef's fate. It was only the second day after our arrival." Sipping water from her glass, Elsa glanced over at Marissa, who nodded to her.

"Kat and I were standing at the gate, waiting for our work detail to begin, when I saw another group being led down a different path. They were the infirm, the lame, the mentally ill, and the aged. Some were carried by others, some were prodded with guns, while others simply stared ahead as if welcoming the end of their ordeal."

"Where are they going?" Katya asked a woman standing next to her.

"To be gassed," came the answer without emotion. "That's where Himmler intends on sending all of the Jews and other enemies of the Reich."

Elsa turned and cocked her head. "What do you mean, gassed?"

The woman glared at her as if her questions were ridiculously stupid.

"Killed, eliminated, destroyed."

"But this is a work camp."

"Don't be a fool. Most Jews that come here are gassed right away. Only a slim ten, maybe fifteen, percent live."

Kat turned to Elsa just in time to keep her from fainting to the ground.

"You're lying," Katya cried, fanning Elsa.

"I wish I were. Less than forty percent of the incoming Jews live to see the next day, and if you're a male, forget it. I lost four brothers, a father, and five uncles already." The woman's voice was cold and without inflection.

"Papa," Elsa whimpered, looking out at the straggling crowd being shepherded across the path.

"Oh, Elsa, I'm so sorry."

Elsa suddenly rose up and stood straight. "What about the children? Surely they do not murder them as well?"

The woman's hardened eyes turned to the ground. "Before I came, I heard rumors that Hitler was killing children in hospitals."

Elsa's trembling hand covered her mouth as a short cry slid out. "Not Josef," she said, burying her face in Katya's shoulder. "Not my Josef."

Elsa stopped and wiped a tear away with her handkerchief. She saw that many of the women in the audience were wiping their own eyes as well.

"Shortly after that, I learned about the experiments Doktor Mengele was performing on Jewish women, and I saw how the guards used his name as a weapon of fear. The threat of being sent to him was felt by everyone in the camp, and even Yvonne trembled at the sound of his name.

"So when Marissa finally saw me, she was seeing a woman who understood just how much it would take to survive this awful existence. No longer was I a baker's daughter keeping house for her Papa. Now, I was number 12575, determined to keep Himmler, Mengele, and all the rest of the Nazis from ever reading my arm. Because once they read your arm, you were selected for either the showers or, worse yet, one of Mengele's sick experiments."

"Elsa, are you awake?"

Elsa, now a light sleeper, rolled over to find Yvonne standing at their bunk.

"What do you want?" Elsa whispered, afraid to startle Katya.

"I need to speak with you."

Reluctantly climbing out of bed, Elsa wondered if Yvonne wanted more from their bargain than what they agreed upon.

Following Yvonne to the back of the barracks, Elsa wondered if she wasn't better off turning back and going to bed. It had been two weeks since she had visited Marissa. Maybe Yvonne wished for more favors.

Sitting on the floor with her back against the wall, Yvonne motioned for Elsa to do the same. As the searchlight beam traced its usual pattern, Yvonne turned to Elsa and sighed.

"I sense that you neither fear me nor hate me as the others do."

Elsa shrugged. "There is no energy or room for hate, Yvonne. Besides, I am not your judge."

Yvonne turned away and looked out into the darkness. "Do you understand that I do what I do in order to survive?"

Elsa nodded and noted the pain in Yvonne's voice. "Isn't that what we're all doing?"

"I don't mean to hurt anyone. It's just my job to keep them and me alive."

"Why are you telling me this? You do not need my forgiveness. You have done nothing to me." Elsa thought she saw a tear form in the corner of Yvonne's eye.

"I . . . I'm telling you this so you will understand that I am not some kind of monster. Oh, I know that most Kapos are brutal and cruel, and some of them enjoy it, but I . . . I do not. It is an act."

"Well, it is a good one, Yvonne. Most of the women are very frightened of you."

Yvonne suddenly turned to Elsa and grabbed her hand. "But don't you see, it is a good act because . . . before the war, I was an actress."

Elsa tried not to look surprised.

"I am not as mean as everyone believes me to be. But when I arrived, I soon understood what I needed to do to survive. I like to believe that my harshness spares lives."

"I'm sure it has." Elsa's tone was soft.

"I saw that Kapos got better treatment and were entrusted with more than just their own lives. And . . . and I knew I was too soft to survive without special treatment. I . . . I am not a very strong woman."

"So you put on the mask of Kapo?"

Yvonne bowed her head. "I had to."

"And now that everyone hates and fears you, you no longer want it?"

"Oh no, nothing like that. I am not strong enough still. Acting is the only way I am going to stay alive in here. It's also the only way I have of keeping others alive."

Elsa could tell by the shift in her voice whom she was speaking of. "Do you mean Katya?"

Yvonne nodded. "I am worried for her."

Elsa had seen it, too. Katya had lost too much weight and was jaundiced. She would not take any of the food offered to her, nor would she slow down when working. Elsa wondered which Katya feared worse; being kicked by Yvonne or sleeping with her.

"She has lost too much weight too fast. I've seen it happen before, and women as small as her do not last long."

Elsa said nothing; only feeling the fear of losing Katya to the ovens gripped her throat like a Nazi's black leather glove.

"What is it you want me to do? I have offered her my food, and she will not take it."

"As well she shouldn't. You need to keep up your own strength as well. Once one gets sick in here, there's little we can do to save them."

"Then what do we do?"

Reaching into her worn jacket, Yvonne pulled out half a potato and a palmful of bread. "I want you to give these to her. Make her eat."

Elsa stared, mouth watering, at the treasures in Yvonne's hand. Then she looked up to Yvonne, wondering what price Katya would have to pay for real food.

"I want nothing in return," Yvonne said, as if hearing her thoughts. "I simply do no want to watch her die."

75

"Surely you don't think she will accept these from you without feeling—"

Yvonne waved her off. "Don't tell her they are from me. She would not take them if you did. Tell her your friend sent them over. Say whatever will make her eat. If you don't, she will die."

Elsa took the jewels gently in her cracked hands and nodded.

"But be careful, Elsa. The others might know, and then we'd all feel the Logiernfuhren's wrath."

"I'll be careful."

Yvonne wiped her cheek with the back of her hand, and Elsa studied her face in the shadows of the night. She must have been close to beautiful a lifetime ago when she walked her tall, regal body across the stage. Her chiseled nose and prominent chin displayed a fearlessness and courage that said she seldom doubted herself. But Elsa was beginning to see otherwise. She was a woman, just like the rest of them, fighting to stay alive so she could see the day the barbed wire fences fell down and they were reunited with family and friends. She was another human being trying to survive in conditions so subhuman few animals could survive. Seeing her now, vulnerable, afraid, willing to help someone she cared for, Elsa felt a tiny, warm spot in her heart for Yvonne.

"Elsa, I will hand what I can to you every other night. Just stay in your bunk and do not say a word."

Elsa nodded. "I would wish you live through this, Yvonne, so that I can tell people what a brave and wonderful woman you truly are."

"Thank you."

"No, thank you. And some day, when she isn't so afraid of you, Katya will come to realize that you care deeply for her."

"I hope so."

Padding through the dark, Elsa quietly climbed back to the bunk.

"Katya, are you awake?"

Katya rolled over to face her, and Elsa could hear a slight rattling sound as she breathed.

76

"Elsa, are you okay?"

Elsa nodded. "Wake up. I have something for you."

Chapter Twenty

Werner examined the dress carefully. This was the second time she checked Marissa's progress.

"*Unglaublich,*" she murmured. "Unbelievable. You did not lie. These two dresses were made by the same hand."

Marissa nodded, unsmiling. "You have a discerning eye, ma'am. Both were sewn by my own hand."

Werner frowned and studied Marissa for a moment. "I see. So someone had you sew this dress for them back at your home?"

Marissa swallowed audibly as Fritzi glowered at her, and Stefanie and Claudia waited for her answer. Slowly, Marissa shook her head.

"Then you lie."

"I do not. No one had me sew it. I . . . designed it myself."

Fritzi stepped forward. "She lies. I've seen her work, and I would know—"

Werner held up a gloved hand. "Silence."

Fritzi froze.

"You tell me you thought the design of this dress up in your head?"

Marissa nodded slowly. "Yes, Logiernfuhren Werner. I have been designing dresses for some time. Many have been sent to Berlin."

"I see. That will be all." Wheeling about, Werner marched out the door carrying the two dresses with her.

"You are a fool, Kowalski," Fritzi grumbled, stepping close to her.

"Leave her alone, Fritzi," Stefanie warned.

"You're all too stupid to see what Kowalski is doing! She wants the creature comforts and better condition of working for the SS wives, and where will that leave the rest of you?"

"That's not so," Marissa returned.

"Of course it is. You just don't have the nerve to come out and say it. Well, it'll be a cold day in hell before I let Werner give you a ride through easy street, you fucking Pollock."

"Back off, Fritzi. You know as well as I do that the Nazis get the best of us. If Marissa is the best, she deserves those tiny luxuries the SS wives hand out. So give it a rest, will you?" Stefanie waited for Fritzi's reply, but Marissa turned away and took Stefanie with her.

"Mark my words, Sukova! You and your little pack of thieves are going to find yourselves inhaling gas. So you'd better watch your step."

Walking into the storeroom, Marissa turned to Stefanie. "What did she mean? 'You and your little pack of thieves?'"

Stefanie shrugged. "Who knows? She's so stupid she can't even talk right. Don't worry about her."

"How can I not? She controls everything we do."

A sly smile crept across Stefanie's face. "Not everything, and not me, ever."

Marissa shook her head. "I don't know what you have on her, but whatever it is, it's big."

Winking at Claudia, Stefanie's smile grew. "You could say that, my friend."

Claudia shook her head. "She means you trouble, Marissa. Unlike Stef, here, you should watch how often you cross her. Fritzi is nothing if not full of vengeance. Just be careful you don't overheat her."

Watching Stefanie and Claudia walk back into the warehouse, Marissa wondered, how hot is hot when you're in hell?

Chapter Twenty-One

Two days later, the door banged open, and Werner walked in with another guard. As women scrambled to the floor, Werner made her way to Marissa, who stood with her left arm bare and extended.

"You are to come with me," Werner commanded before heading for the door. The other guard grabbed Marissa's arm and hauled her out.

Once outside, Werner addressed her. "I have checked your papers and shown your dresses to three wives of prominent SS officials. The women have requested to see you about designing apparel for them. You will go with Corporal Schneider, here, to talk with them about their wishes, take their measurements, and answer any questions they might have. Do you understand?"

Marissa inhaled deeply, knowing the enormous risk she was taking with her next words. "I will do what you ask on one condition."

Werner's countenance was caught somewhere between anger and amusement. "You wish to bargain when you have nothing but your life with which to pay?"

Marissa nodded. "You are correct when you say I have nothing. What better time to try to get something. There is something in the bargain for you as well." Her cards were on the table, and the lone chip she held delicately in her palm was her life.

Werner stiffened at the obvious implication. "What makes you think I should care what the SS think of me?"

Marissa was treading lightly now. "You do not like it here anymore than we do. A recommendation by an SS officer is your ticket out. A ticket, I might add, that will be cut and sewn by me."

Werner mulled this over. "Your insolence could have you killed. You must certainly be aware of that?"

Marissa nodded once. "I am."

"And that does not frighten you?"

Marissa shook her head. "If I was dealing with an irrational being, Logiernfuhren, it might. But I have services to offer that you want, and I ask for so little in return."

Werner studied her a moment as if weighing, on the spot, the value of her life and the import of her skills. "I was not aware there were any Poles with such courage, Kowalski. You do your people a service."

Marissa said nothing.

"Very well then, what is it that would be so important to you that you would risk your life?"

"More milk, ma'am, for the women in the warehouse."

Werner looked bemused. "Milk? Did you say milk?"

"Yes, ma'am."

Considering this for a moment, Werner finally jerked her head at Schneider, who scribbled a memo.

"You will have your extra rations of milk. But should any of the SS wives be displeased with your work, you will pay for that milk with your blood."

"I understand."

"Do you?" Werner asked, seemingly of no one. "I wonder." Then, turning back to Marissa, she shook her head. "Marissa Kowalski, you are either the biggest fool I have ever met or one of the bravest souls in Auschwitz. I just don't know which."

Following them through the compound, Marissa sent up a silent prayer and muttered, "Neither do I."

Chapter Twenty-Two

"Well?" Stefanie's gray eyes bore through her.

Marissa shrugged. "I took their measurements, spoke of color combinations and flattering designs, and then left."

"Is that all?"

"Yes. They were like any other women coming into a shop for a fitting. Only, one of them was large enough to take up the fabric of two women."

Stefanie's eyes were riveted to Marissa. "There's something else. Something you're not telling me."

Marissa moved to her machine. "I think I saw Elsa."

"Really? Where?"

"Just outside the gate. They were digging some sort of irrigation canal. When I looked up, she was resting against her shovel with her arms holding up a tiny woman. I think it was her. It was so hard to tell. She's so . . . thin."

Stefanie laid a comforting hand on her shoulder. "We're all thin, M. It's the nature of the beast in here."

"But we're not that skinny. She's emaciated."

"Count your blessings, M. We're not nearly as bad off as many of the others. The women who work the details have a much harder time of it than we do."

Marissa stared down at the needle as it plunged up and down, up and down. "I must see her."

Stefanie shook her head. "I had a feeling you'd say something like that."

"Stef, I must."

"It would be an awful risk, M. It would be better if you just looked after yourself."

Marissa turned on her. "Is that where all of this leads us? There's Jew beating up Jew, gypsy stealing from gypsy, and Pole fighting Pole. No wonder there are so few guards needed to run this place. We're too busy lording

82

over each other for a few scraps of bread. It makes me sick!"

"It's survival of the fittest, M., pure and simple. Stay fit and live."

"Not so, Stef. Even in the survival of the fittest, the weak don't devour the weak. If we would just band together and forget about our cultural differences—"

"It'll never happen. Stop dreaming, M., and join the reality of it all. Take care of number one and live to see the end of the war. Stop worrying so much about your friend and focus on keeping yourself together."

Marissa slowly reached out and touched Stefanie's cheek. "I cannot do that. If I lose my humanity and still live, I might as well be dead."

Stefanie's eyes softened. "There's a dreamer in every bunch. I guess I just thought that you Poles dealt only with the concrete."

Marissa grinned. "We do, my friend, when we're dealing with Czechs. The rest of the time, we pursue the more sophisticated abstract."

The two women looked into each other's faces and felt the silent understanding that there was no "right way" to survive the brutal nightmare, except the way each individual spirit could manage without being pushed over the brink of despair.

For now, Marissa would appease the SS wives and keep Fritzi and Werner off everyone's backs. Who knew how she would handle tomorrow?

Chapter Twenty-Three

It took Marissa a few days to design and make the three dresses for the SS wives, and while it was a nice change to sew with some creativity, she would not forsake her friends in their effort to meet their quota. The extra ration of milk lifted morale, and Marissa felt that the overall benefit from it was seen in the quality of the work as well. Marissa was not the least bit surprised when Fritzi claimed that it was she who requested the extra milk for the "fine work they were doing."

"That lying son-of-a-bitch," Stefanie growled, finishing a pair of work overalls.

"It's not important, Stef. Let it go."

"But, M., don't you see what that cow has done? I have half a mind to—"

"Marissa is right, Stef. Forget about it."

Both Marissa and Stefanie were surprised by Claudia's statement. Tall, lean, clear-eyed Claudia seemed to speak only when spoken to. Seldom did she step out on her own.

"Leave Fritzi alone, Stef, or they'll be carting you out of here."

"She'll do no such thing."

"I don't want you taking that chance," Claudia's voice raised a little. "You take enough chances already."

Stefanie shrugged. "Only enough to make a difference. But don't sweat so much, C. If M. doesn't care that the fat cow stole her glory, then neither do I."

Marissa nodded, pretending to understand the secret she and Claudia so obviously shared.

"Besides, if I get too far out of line, then I have to answer to C., and she can be a real bear sometimes."

Claudia only nodded and looked down at the material running through her hands.

"Did you two meet in here?" Marissa asked.

Stefanie nodded. "One by one, my friends were selected until I was the only one left. My dearest friend, may she rest in peace, was taken to Barracks 11."

Marissa felt her blood go cold. "Mengele?" she whispered, as if the saying of his name would conjure up Satan himself.

Stefanie nodded. "She returned to the warehouse in a pitiful state and died in my arms days later. Only C. was able to pry my arms from her withered and tortured body. I was in shock for a week, with only C. moving me from place to place like a puppet. She kept me going."

Claudia looked over at Stefanie and grinned sheepishly. "I'd been in her shoes not two days before, when my mother was taken from me. I knew the pain. I . . . felt Stefanie's."

Marissa stopped her sewing and rubbed a drop of sweat off her forehead. "I have heard of some of the experiments. I'm sorry."

Bowing her head, Stefanie nodded. "She did not die alone, nor did she die in vain. I swore to her that I would live so that I could tell her story across the world. Maybe I'll write a book about this place, who knows?"

Pulling the cloth through her machine, Marissa leaned over and held Stefanie's hand. "Your friend's death; is that the reason you are so cold and matter-of-fact?"

Stefanie said nothing, but Marissa saw Claudia nodding her head.

"I'm truly sorry."

"Aren't we all? M., this place has branded us forever. Getting close to someone, really knowing who they are, is too much of a risk here. And why should I, when everyone I loved is dead? How much spiritual death can a being take before their own soul crumbles and dies?" Standing up, Stefanie tossed the overalls into a pile. "I take care of me, M., and if that's cold and matter-of-fact, then so be it. But it's the only way any of us will ever get out of here. Look out for number one. I suggest you do the same." With that, she walked out.

"I really made her mad, didn't I?"

Claudia shook her head. "It's not you. Stefanie wants to love, she wants to care, but she cannot bring herself to any longer, and I think it frightens her."

Marissa felt a chill run up her arms. "What do we have, Claudia, if we don't have love?"

Her eyes following Stefanie out the door, Claudia shrugged. "I wish I knew, Marissa. I really do."

Chapter Twenty-Four

They had been in Auschwitz over a month, and autumn was setting in. Marissa had seen the SS wives on three occasions, and they seemed genuinely pleased with her efforts. The heavyset wife even gave Marissa a chocolate bar for her work and told her that her first dress was the envy of the other women. As always, when one of them offered Marissa a token, she dropped it into her pocket for later. She may work for these women, but she wasn't about to gorge herself like some starving animal in front of them.

The hardest part of it all was remembering that these women, who talked to her and treated her like a servant instead of a prisoner of war, were wives of prominent Nazi officials; they were, by all rights, enemies. But try as she may, Marissa could not find it in her heart to hate these women, nor could she find justification to do so. The difficult part was that her friends in the warehouse expected her to despise them, and they taunted her about it every time she would leave the warehouse for a fitting.

"Don't let them bother you," Claudia said one night.

Marissa shrugged. "I try not to, but it seems as if there's so much hate. Who has the time or energy for such feelings?"

Claudia rolled over and put an arm around Marissa. "Revenge has its price, Marissa. Some of these women survive daily on the food of vengeful thoughts. Don't think less of them for it."

"I don't. I just wish they would leave me out of it."

"They will." Claudia gazed hard at Marissa. "I feel there is more on your mind than the SS women."

Marissa sighed. Claudia, the silent one, who watched Stefanie with eagle eyes and protected everyone from Fritzi's wrath, seemed to have the pulse of her every emotion, and it wasn't without a little discomfort that she would find Claudia looking at her whenever she was feeling some deep-seated emotion. This instance was no exception.

"It's Elsa."

Claudia scooted a little closer.

"I saw her again today. She gets thinner and thinner, and I always see her with that short woman. Who is she, anyway?"

"Do you want me to have Stefanie find out?"

Marissa pinched the bridge of her nose. "God, do I sound stupid, or what? No, Claudia, there's no need to spy on her. It's just . . ."

"Just that you are jealous and wish to find out if you should be or not?"

Marissa peered through the darkness. She wasn't even sure Claudia was looking at her. "Something like that. Am I being foolish?"

"We are all foolish, Marissa. When will you learn that the only reality in this place exists within our own minds? You must stop judging yourself by past standards and learn to adapt to this chaotic world. If you don't, you will go mad or die."

Marissa leaned on her elbow and strained to see some feature of Claudia's face in the semi-darkness of the room. "Is that what you do? Is that why you're so quiet most of the time?"

"It's what I learned to do. Everything is out of balance in here; nothing is as it should be. The only way I handle the abnormalities of this place is by focusing on the truths I know in my own mind. That's what saves me."

"I don't know if I have that kind of inner strength."

"Of course you do. You just need to find a safer place for your emotions, that's all. So what if your Elsa has found someone to share her pain with? Are you so petty that you would begrudge her that?"

Opening her mouth to snap at Claudia, Marissa was suddenly struck with the truthfulness of her question. "You're right. I keep making value judgments—"

"In a place where the only valuable thing is staying alive. Stop torturing yourself every day, Marissa. If you need to see her, we'll see what Stefanie can do. See her, tell her everything you would want her to know before you die, and leave it at that. Get on with the business of self-survival."

Lying back down, Marissa nodded. "Do you think Stefanie can help?"

At the mention of Stefanie's name, the bunk suddenly started to rock.

"Did someone mention my name in vain?" Stefanie asked, climbing into the bunk from one of her late-night rendezvous.

"I was just telling Marissa that you would help her if she wanted to see Elsa."

"Hmph," Stefanie offered, crawling next to Claudia. "The rumor has it that they're stepping up the killings. It looks like things are only going to get worse for a while."

Closing her eyes to the harsh sounds of the night, Marissa thought about the war raging on the outside. And as it blistered through Europe, the war on the inside was intensifying as well. Piles of naked corpses were stacked higher than ever; their rotting, rigid bodies attracted hordes of flies and other disease-carrying insects. There were rumors that Mengele was actually injecting people with diseases and that was the reason the guards failed to move the emaciated, naked piles of decaying flesh. Whatever the rumors were, the death machines were speeding up while the burial teams were slowing down. And those weren't the only changes felt by the women.

The change in weather brought about other changes as well. More people were starving to death and were usually found naked and dead in the morning. As snow started falling, and the weather turned cold and miserable, frostbite claimed body parts like some evil-spirited cannibal.

"Why do you suppose?" Marissa whispered, suddenly feeling silly for worrying about Elsa's new friend.

"They're bringing Jews in from all over Europe now. Greeks, Danes, Slavs, you name it, they're here. The more they bring in—"

"The more they destroy."

"Exactly. The minute one of us becomes expendable, we're dead."

A cold flurry tumbled down Marissa's spine.

"I also heard that Werner finally got her transfer."

"Really?"

"Thanks to you, M. You're quite a success. Even Fritzi had to admit that you've made a difference."

Marissa did not respond. The only real success for her in the camp would be to survive and walk out with Elsa next to her. "If they are moving up more quickly, then—"

"No you don't," Stefanie interrupted.

"Yes." Marissa's voice was firm. "Yes, I do. And soon. I don't know where you go at night or what it is you do, but surely there must be some way of getting me over to see her."

Stefanie sighed loudly. "It would be too dangerous."

"I can pay."

Stefanie rose on one elbow. "What?"

Marissa lowered her voice. "I said I can pay." Reaching into her pocket, Marissa pulled out three chocolate bars.

"Don't tell me . . . the SS women?"

Marissa nodded. "Don't be angry."

"Angry? How could I be angry? You're finally starting to get it." Pulling Marissa to her, Stefanie snuggled up to her. "Put those away. I know a camp prostitute who will do anything for chocolate."

"You mean that gypsy woman with the sores on her legs?" Marissa cringed at the memories of seeing this woman on her hands and knees while a fat, bare-assed guard humped over her panting and wheezing.

"Yeah, her. If we can bribe her off, we should be able to buy enough time to get you over there."

Marissa pulled away. "We?"

"Don't be ridiculous. You'd never make it on your own. I know how this place works at night. Leave it to me."

Marissa nodded and dropped the bars back in her pocket.

"Just tell me one thing, M. Why is she so important to you? I mean, you've done nothing but stare out the window and worry about her since you got here. What, exactly, is she to you?"

Remembering the savage beating she watched not long ago of four men wearing pink triangles, Marissa looked hard into Stefanie's eyes. At night, her gray eyes were almost white, like wolves' eyes that shone through the darkness.

"M., did you hear me?"

Marissa nodded slowly, suddenly feeling miles away from herself. So far, she had witnessed the guards deny them of food, clothing, warmth, medicine, shoes, and bathroom facilities. They stripped them of their freedom, their health, their dignity, and with the exception of the felt triangles and stars, of their identity. She would not allow them to deny her the love that fed her spirit.

"She's my lover."

"I figured it was something like that."

"Does it bother you?"

Stefanie laughed. "Nothing anyone does in here bothers me anymore. You're luckier than most of us, M. You've still got someone to love. The rest just isn't important."

Marissa nodded and laid her head down. "I suppose you're right."

"Of course I'm right. Now get some sleep."

Feeling the mist of sleep creep over her mind, Marissa kept hearing Stefanie's voice.

"You're luckier than most of us."

Luckier?

Just how important a role did Lady Luck play in the lives of those in a death camp? Marissa was soon to find out.

Chapter Twenty-Five

"The gypsy glutton has agreed to keep the guard busy for fifteen minutes. She says that's about all he's worth." Stefanie's eyes twinkled. "That gives us about five going, five coming back, and three or four once we're there. I know it's not much, but it's the best I can do."

"It is a gift I gratefully accept. Just to see her for a moment, to hold her close . . ."

Stefanie playfully punched her shoulder. "I get the picture."

"I'm . . . sorry."

"Don't apologize. Maybe I'm just envious that you are still able to feel love, while I feel nothing but a stirring numbness."

Marissa's eyebrows raised. The question on her lips had fermented long enough. "Is there another reason why you don't criticize my feelings for another woman?"

Stefanie's eyes did not blink. "No. Why should I? There is precious little of it in the first place."

"Do you . . . do you love Claudia?"

This made Stefanie smile. "I care for C., but I don't know if I love her. If love is about self-sacrifice, then I don't. I take care of me first."

"If you care for her, then you do feel."

Stefanie shrugged. "I suppose I do. But it is too dangerous to do so. If it came down to my stomach or Claudia's life, I would have no other choice than to take care of the former."

Marissa turned on her. "I do not believe that! You care for her very much. I can tell."

"Then you do not look closely enough. I don't remember what love feels like anymore."

"Well, she loves you."

Stefanie looked up, her face a mask. "She confuses love with admiration. C. loves my strength, my courage, my—"

Marissa stopped her by placing her hand over her mouth. "She loves who you are, Stefanie Sukova. I know. I can read it in her eyes. So could you, if you slowed down to look at her long enough."

"Maybe I choose not to see."

"There is no shame in accepting her love, my friend, even if you only accept it in your heart."

Stefanie reached up to touch Marissa's face. "You are an incredible woman to find an ounce of goodness in such a dark place. Before you came, I thought only dark thoughts and saw myself growing into a block of ice."

"Are you saying that you've thawed?"

Stefanie's eyes watered. "Thawing. I just hope I don't curse you for it someday."

"And Claudia?"

Impatiently wiping her eyes, Stefanie nodded. "I can accept the love she feels for me in my heart, but . . . I'm afraid I simply do not have the capacity to love as you do, M. Forgive me." Hopping off the bunk, Stefanie's attitude changed like a flipped coin. "Got the chocolate?"

Marissa felt in her pocket and nodded.

"Good. Now, no matter what happens, let me do the talking, and don't ever run. No matter how scared you are, don't run."

Marissa quietly followed Stefanie out the door. Immediately, the cold night air stung her face and throat, but she ignored the icicle pricks stabbing through her clothes.

Walking through the compound at night was an eerie experience. The searchlights swept across the grounds in spasmodic crisscross patterns, the screams from the medical barracks reverberated through the air, and scores of grunting and groaning noises could be heard from ominous black shadows swaying and dancing beneath the harsh glare of the roving lights.

"This is it," Stefanie whispered, pointing to Elsa's barracks. "You have four minutes. I will count time and knock twice when you should leave. Do not hesitate when you hear the knock. Being on the compound at night is quite a risk. If you don't come immediately, I will leave you to find your own way back. Understand?"

Marissa nodded and reached out to touch Stefanie's head. "Thank you."

"Go."

Opening the door, Marissa was somewhat surprised to see that all of the women were in bed, and most, if not all, were asleep. Moving through the barracks, Marissa could not believe the horrible stench of the place. It smelled of vomit, urine, and body odor of the worst degree. Not even the cold air could douse the smell hanging in the air like cheap cigar smoke. Compared to this barracks, hers was a castle.

Gazing down at the rows and rows of bunks, Marissa felt an immediate sense of hopelessness. She would never find Elsa in only four minutes.

"Psst."

Marissa ducked and looked over her shoulder and into the darkness.

"Elsa?" Marissa whispered, stepping to the edge of the shadowy darkness. She could see no one.

"You came." Stepping out of the shadow like a ghost from a closet, Elsa's thin frame floated over to Marissa. "I knew you'd come." Throwing her arms around Marissa's neck, Elsa hugged her tightly.

"How did you know?"

"Your friend sent word. She told me to wait for you. Oh, Mari, how I have lived for this moment."

Slowly pulling away, Marissa took Elsa's face in her hands and gazed into her sunken eyes. Were these the same eyes that danced whenever she walked into the bakery? Were these cracked lips the same silky ones that used to caress her body? Was this shrunken skeleton of a woman the same woman as the one with the luscious hips and mounds of breasts? In the blink of Time's eye, Elsa had transformed from a rose to the mere shadow of its stem.

"I had to see you." Marissa kissed Elsa's forehead. "I watch you sometimes from the warehouse, and I've noticed . . ."

"That I'm a scarecrow without stuffing? They work us to death in the field, my darling. But that is not important. What's important is us." Without even checking around first, Elsa placed her lips on Marissa's and tenderly kissed her.

"Am I still the one?" Marissa asked before she could stop herself.

Elsa cocked her head in that familiar way. "Of course you are. What makes you think otherwise?"

Marissa shrugged, wishing she had not asked. "That dwarf of a woman always around you. I thought—"

"Kat? Oh, Mari, don't tell me you thought—" Elsa covered her mouth and then pulled Marissa to her. "She is my dearest friend, without whom I would be lost. But that is all."

Marissa lowered her face into Elsa's neck. "I feel ridiculous for asking. Forgive me."

"There's nothing to forgive, my love. It just shows how much you still love me. I need to know you care, that you still feel. So many of the women around us are empty shells waiting for their number to be called. As long as you feel, as long as you love, you'll fight to stay alive. That is most important. Do not ever apologize for feeling, my love."

Marissa kissed her once more. "I thought I would be the one to tell you to hang on."

"I have changed a great deal since we walked through those gates. I am not the helpless person I once was. I have learned what it takes to survive this place, and I know it starts in here." Elsa pointed to her heart. "I live to be with you, Mari. I want to make it through this so we may live out our dreams. It is our love that keeps me strong."

Marissa looked at Elsa and lightly touched her cheek with the back of her hand. "You do not look strong, Sweetness."

"My body is a bit frail, but my spirit is strong. Don't judge my abilities to stay alive on looks alone."

Marissa gazed into Elsa's eyes, and the attitude she displayed threw water on her burning doubt. Elsa had indeed changed.

"But you will stay alive." It was not a question.

Elsa took her in her arms once more and kissed her with the same passion she only dreamt about. "Yes, Mari, and so will you. It is our goal, and we owe it to each other to fight death to the bitter end."

Suddenly, there were two sharp raps at the door.

"I must go. I love you, Sweetness. You, only you, and always you."

Elsa kissed Marissa's lips once more. "And know that I return that love, no matter what your eyes tell you." Taking Marissa's hand, Elsa kissed it. "And continue doing your best work. I have heard of your work for the SS women, and I applaud that. No matter what, Mari, don't waver on your convictions." Kissing her palm, Elsa released her hand. "I'll love you forever." Slipping back into the darkness, Elsa was gone.

Again came the knocks.

"Here I am," Marissa whispered, opening the door.

"About time. Come on."

Once they were back in their own bunk, Marissa let out a painful sigh. For a long, long time, she laid there, saying nothing, simply feeling worlds of emotions she did not know existed within her. Finally, Stefanie rolled over and pulled her close.

"How did it go, M.?"

"It was wonderful to see her."

"But?"

Marissa shrugged. "But she's a walking corpse. Her ribs poke through her clothes."

"So do yours."

"But not as much."

"So? What are you trying to say?"

"Have you ever wondered if we're all dying and we don't even know it?"

Stefanie nodded.

"If you knew, without a doubt, that you were dying, what would you do differently?"

"I'd try to escape."

Her answer did not surprise Marissa.

"What's this all about, M.? Don't tell me—"

"No, I'm not going to try to escape. Not from the camp at least."

Stefanie sat up. "What then?"

Marissa sighed again. She had thought about it when she first arrived. It was a thought she had been entertaining for some time. "I have decided that I cannot stay here. I cannot continue wondering whether or not she's made it through the day."

"Careful, M. I don't like the direction this is heading."

"Stef, I thought we lived like vermin, but compared to them, this place is a palace. We get better clothes, better food, better working conditions. You know what they have? A sewer with a roof on it."

"But they're making the best of it, M., just like the rest of us."

"Right. While I'm pocketing chocolate bars like someone's pet dog, Elsa is fading into nothingness."

"You can't compare work loads, M. We have a skill. They don't. It's as easy as that."

"There's nothing easy about that. I can't believe that even in this hellhole there's a caste system. It makes me sick. Why is that so hard for us to see?"

"Because it's not true. We're better off not only because we are skilled, but because we aren't Jews. That's good news to us, M. As long as the Nazis are killing people below us in the pecking order, our lives are prolonged. We'll be one of the last to get it. Be happy for that."

"Forgive me if I don't find that comforting."

Stefanie folded her arms. "So what is it you want?"

Marissa closed her eyes and laid her arm across her face. "I've decided that I would rather die with her than live without her."

Stefanie's eyes widened. "Do you know what you're doing? Do you have any idea how hard life is outside?"

Marissa nodded. "Harder physically than emotionally. I look at it as a trade-off I'm willing to live with."

"That is, if you live." Stefanie shook her head. "Is there anything I can say that will change your mind?"

Marissa shook her head. "I'm afraid not. Elsa said not to waver on my convictions. I could not live with myself if she died while I worked away making fancy dresses for chocolate bars."

"Then I wish you luck, my friend, because luck is the only factor in surviving the trenches."

Rolling over with her back to Stefanie, Marissa exhaled loudly. Now that she knew what she had to do, she had only to figure out how to do it.

Chapter Twenty-Six

Elsa moved back over to the podium next to Marissa. The shorter of the two women, Elsa always gripped the podium as if doing so lifted her above it. What was most remarkable about them was when their eyes met there was such an exchange of warm commitment that it filled the auditorium.

"What had become painfully aware to Mari was that, in the caste system of the camp, my barracks, and many others like mine, were at the bottom of the rung, clinging to it with fingernails blackened and cracked by too much work and not enough nourishment. The reality of my situation was so startling for her because she finally realized there were actually degrees of hopelessness. And, having seen my degree up close for the first time, she became frightened for me."

Marissa stood next to Elsa and laid her hand across one of the tiny hands clinging to the podium's edge. Even from the back of the room, Marissa's green eyes could be seen, so often saying more than her mouth, so often expressing emotions that were too painful to utter. There was a wisdom, an agelessness that emanated from the cool, confident gaze. Atop one of her marble-like eyes was an eyebrow interrupted by a thick, jagged scar. The abundance of her other eyebrow magnified the size of the two inch mark slithering wickedly down her face.

"There were spiritual patterns everyone of us went through as we survived the day-to-day rigors of the atrocities. Once reality slapped you in the face, we turned inward for survival, understanding that only the strong would live. While we never forgot our loved ones, our main concern was no longer for them, but for our own individual selves. There was tremendous guilt that went along with this, and often, guilt acted as the agent of destruction. Elie Wiesel, who wrote the wonderful novel Night, *even spoke of a time when he wished that his father was dead so that he could focus solely on himself." Marissa wiped her short gray bangs away from her forehead before continuing.*

"The next pattern came when you realized that you could survive the day's hardships and the night's cold. Some of us started looking outside ourselves again; we started choosing to

help others make it along with us. I had seen, firsthand, what happened to those who shut off their emotions completely. I had looked into those gray eyes of Stefanie Sukova enough to know the damage it could do to be emotionally dead inside. I did not want that to happen to me.

"It was then that I made my decision to leave the warehouse and live the rest of my days with Elsa." Marissa stepped back behind Elsa, who leaned into the microphone.

"It became clear to me the night she visited that we were living in two separate hells. It was odd. So many women resented others they felt had it easier. Easier. There was no such thing in a death camp. Is the prisoner who has a cell with a window freer than the one who doesn't? It was all relative, and I wasn't about to begrudge Mari or anyone else for their manner of survival. If you could escape death every night, then who was to judge how you did it?

"It was almost three weeks after our visit that my barracks first gazed into the face of the Angel of Death."

"Up! Get up! Mengele is coming!"

The name brought chills of fear to Elsa's body. Thus far, they had only heard rumors about the Angel of Death. But now, now he was alighting in their midst, ready to pluck some of them like unripened grapes.

When the doors swung open, a rigid figure dressed in a crisp, black SS uniform stepped in. With him, the frigid morning air permeated the room and their flimsy clothing.

Mengele walked past the first dozen women holding their left arms outstretched without so much as a glance. The two guards with him held clipboards from which one read the numbers and the other looked at their arms.

Next to her, Elsa could hear Katya's deep breaths as he approached. He seemed faintly interested in her, and in one large step, stood before her.

Elsa felt her legs tremble as she stared straight ahead. It was thought that if Mengele looked into your eyes, you would not live long. Now, as he stood so close to her, she could smell antiseptic and a strange smelling cologne hovering like a dark cloud. The evil she had heard about dripped off his demeanor like hot, greasy tar.

"Are you a dwarf?" he asked Katya, looking, but not looking at her.

"*Nein, Herr Doktor.*"

"You certainly are short enough to be, don't you think?"

"I don't know, Herr Doktor, I have never seen one.

For the longest time, Mengele studied Katya, weighing the life and death decisions on his own twisted scale.

"Perhaps—"

"Excuse me, Herr Doktor," Yvonne said suddenly. "The twins you seek are three bunks down."

Mengele looked up from Katya and looked, but didn't look, at Yvonne. It was Mengele's eyes that were his most frightening feature; the way he never really looked at anyone, but sort of around them; unless, that is, he had selected you for death. Then those eyes would penetrate to the back of your skull like a steel rod being driven through your brain.

"Good!" Turning briskly away from Katya, Mengele and the guards walked down the aisle until they came to Hannah and Gwen, two fraternal twins. Whatever conversation he had with them, Elsa could not hear, and they were escorted out the back way shortly after. As Mengele walked past Katya, he stopped suddenly and turned to her. Elsa heard Katya's breath catch in her throat.

"I am not convinced you are not a dwarf. I will check your papers when I return to my office. If you are, and have lied, I will make you wish you had never been born." With the snap of his head, Mengele turned and walked out the door.

"Oh . . . my . . . God," Katya murmured, sinking to her knees.

Elsa helped her to her feet and laid her on the bottom bunk. Her whole body was like a block of ice.

"It's okay, Kat. He is gone. It's over."

Still trembling, Katya looked up into Elsa's eyes. "I'm afraid, Elsa, that it is just the beginning for me."

Elsa cocked her head in question.

"My real parents died when I was a teenager. They died within three years of each other of a disease that strikes only small people."

Katya's words smashed into Elsa's face.

"Do you mean—"

"Yes, Elsa. That is exactly what I mean. I am a dwarf. A tall one, perhaps, but a dwarf nonetheless."

Chapter Twenty-Seven

"You can't be serious," Stefanie said, pushing the material through the machine.

Marissa broke the thread before nodding. "Why not? Werner is out of here in two days. She got what she wanted, why continue?"

"How about so you can save your life? You only saw the tip of the iceberg when you were in those barracks. Those women die by the dozens every night, and those who don't die of starvation or disease slowly freeze to death. It's sure death, no matter how you look at it."

Marissa looked down at her hands, remembering the hard, calloused hands of Elsa. "All the more reason for me to be with her."

"You're being a fool. With your skill, you could conceivably become one of the SS's private workers. They do it all the time, you know. Prisoners watch their kids, clean their houses, and they live a hell of a lot better off than we do."

Turning, Marissa kept one eye trained on Fritzi, who, of late, started carrying a whip around like many of the guards. Her eye contact prompted Fritzi to wander over.

"Well, Kowalski, it looks as if the easy road is just about at a dead end."

"Stop talking in riddles, Fritzi. What do you want?" Stefanie growled.

"I heard that the SS wives will be going back to Berlin in a few days and will no longer require your services. Looks like it's back to uniforms and gloves for you."

Marissa shrugged. "It's just as well. All that food was giving me a stomach ache."

"What?"

Marissa looked up and smiled. "Gotcha!"

Fritzi stalked off in a huff.

"Not bad, M. I thought I was the only one that could get her goat."

"She's the least of my worries."

Stefanie shook her head. "You are planning on going through with this insanity, aren't you?"

"Tell me, Stef, what kind of life would I live when this was all over and I knew that I had forsaken Elsa for an easier way? How could I live with myself?"

"At least you'd be alive, M. That's the only thing that matters."

"Alive on the outside but dead on the inside is not for me, Stef. I cannot do it. I appreciate your concern, but my mind is made up. Are you going to help me or not?"

Unexpectedly, the next words were not spoken by either of them.

"I'll help you, Marissa," Claudia said, frowning over at Stefanie.

Stefanie threw her hands in the air. "You're both nuts." Then, looking from one face to the other, Stefanie exhaled loudly. "But I'll help. God knows you need all the help you can get."

Marissa smiled gratefully at Claudia. "Good. Now, how do we get me out of here and over to her barracks?"

Stefanie's wolf eyes narrowed. "The only way I can see us managing that piece is to render you incapable of working in here, while still keeping you eligible for other work."

"How would we do that?"

"We've seen it done before. We would have to smash one of your hands."

Claudia nodded. "Fritzi would only let you go if you were of no use to her, and Werner is so happy to be leaving she might agree to have you moved there."

Marissa looked at her right hand. "And if she doesn't move me?"

"You'll be gassed."

The three women did not look at each other as Stefanie said this.

"How can we be sure that I am moved to Elsa's?"

"They're losing the most women. There's room there even with all of the new arrivals. Besides, I think I have what it takes to get you there."

Marissa's eyebrows raised.

"Don't ask, M., because I won't tell you. Just know that it's covered."

"What odds do you give us for success?"

"40-60 against. It all depends on Werner. But you've made her pretty happy, so that's in our favor."

"Marissa, you should give this plenty of thought," Claudia added softly. "We're talking about mutilating your hand. Is it that important to you?"

Marissa locked eyes with Claudia. She knew if anyone understood her motives, it was Claudia. The quiet giant who watched her every move had never questioned Marissa's motives. Perhaps she, more than anyone else, understood the significance of being with Elsa.

"She is that important to me, Claudia."

Stefanie shook her head. "M., if there was another way, I would do it in a second. You're taking an awful risk here."

Claudia nodded. "You do her no service dead, my friend. Perhaps you could wait until we find another way."

Folding the gown she had been working on over her arm, Marissa looked down at it before raising her face toward Stefanie. It had only been a germ of a thought last night, but it was an idea to consider. Perhaps her way out was to confide in someone who was supposed to be her enemy. Perhaps . . .

Leaning over, Marissa nodded to Stefanie. "Maybe there is another way, my gray-eyed friend. Maybe there is."

Chapter Twenty-Eight

The SS wives had not treated her unkindly in all of her dealings with them. With the exception of Frau Hoess, the women were generally pleased with her designs and workmanship. At times, they even talked to her as if she was a peer, and often, whenever two of them would leave the room, the other would ask questions one might ask at a dinner party. In an odd way, Marissa felt sorry for these women. They were pawns in their husbands' power struggles and imprisoned in a system they had no part of constructing.

Waiting for the women to try on their ball gowns, Marissa shifted from foot to foot. The whole way over, all she could think about was having her hand smashed and then being sent to the showers anyway. There was another alternative, equally as risky as Stefanie's, but would allow her to keep both of her hands intact. If she had the opportunity, she would put her own plan into action.

"Oh, Marissa, this is your best yet," came Frau Bruner's voice two seconds before her overweight body appeared. "It's perfect. And it touches me in all of the right places."

"Thank you," Marissa responded, eyes downcast.

"I must concur," came Frau Oberlitz's voice. "Stunning work. Absolutely stunning."

Marissa waited for the shrill voice of Frau Hoess. "Mine's a bit too tight. Perhaps you could let it out some before this evening?"

"Putting on some weight, eh?" Frau Bruner chuckled. She had been the most pleasant of the three women, and when she laughed, which was often, her entire body jiggled.

"Oh, never mind. I was buttoning the wrong buttons."

Frau Oberlitz and Frau Bruner looked at each other and smiled. Their dresses were beautiful on them and accented just the right amount of curves. In Frau Bruner's case, it gave her curves less rotundity.

Looking up at the dresses they wore, Marissa saw that Frau Bruner had put hers on backwards.

"Excuse me, Frau Bruner, but you have the dress on backwards. Your arms go through these."

Looking at the dress, Frau Bruner burst into resounding laughter. "Is that so? Well, of course. Come, my dear, help me wiggle my plump little frame properly into it. Although I must admit it looks stunning on backwards as well."

Stepping into a separate room, Marissa felt her heart pounding. This would be the only chance she would get.

"I understand you will no longer be needing my services."

"If only I could. I can't tell you how many compliments I have received about my new dresses. Even Hermann made a comment. I think it was the first positive thing he has said about me in ten years." Frau Bruner chuckled, making her fat bounce and jiggle. "I'm afraid either our husbands tire of us or," here she lowered her voice and stopped smiling, "we're losing this dumb war and no one wants to admit it. Either way, they're shipping us back to Berlin. Can't say that I'm sorry. Your country is simply too cold for me."

Marissa felt her mouth dry as she pulled one strap over Frau Bruner's shoulder. "Then you won't be returning?"

"No." Frau Bruner turned and eyed Marissa cautiously. "You're awfully chatty this afternoon. Why all these questions?"

Marissa thought about her hand being mutilated and the chance she was about to take with this woman. It would either be a smashed hand or dashed hopes, and either way, she took the risk of being sent to the showers. Still, it was a risk she was willing to take.

"I have enjoyed making these dresses for you, but it has ostracized me from the others."

Frau Bruner now turned fully around to face Marissa.

"I am afraid they will hurt me now that I am no longer of service to the SS."

A wry smile crept across Frau Bruner's jowled face. "Are these other women Jews?"

The question threw Marissa off. "Yes."

"I see. What is it you think I can do for you?"

Swallowing the fear in her throat, Marissa inhaled slowly and plunged in. "There is one barracks that is mostly Polish, and I think I can be of use to them."

Holding up a braceleted arm, Frau Bruner stopped her. "And you would wish me to make this arrangement?" Again, her fat chuckle. "My dear, I am merely the wife of an officer, and not a very good one at that. I have no authority, nor, for that matter, have I any influence over my husband. Now, Frau Hoess—"

"No."

Frau Bruner grinned. "Oh, don't be afraid of her. Her bark is . . . well, let's just say she only bites those in her husband's way. I tell you what. Let me see what I can do. I do have distant relatives who are Poles. I thought I saw one the other day. No matter. I would hate to see a talent such as yours destroyed by the envy of those dirty Jews. I'll look into it. In the meantime, could you possibly make me a jacket to match that dress? I lost the jacket years ago and . . ."

Chapter Twenty-Nine

Four days went by, and Marissa was still sewing away in the warehouse. On the fifth day, she conceded defeat and was getting ready to tell Stefanie that she agreed to go along with their original plan when the door burst open and the new Logiernfuhren strode in, whip in hand. Her stone face and broad shoulders reminded Marissa of a statue she had seen in a park.

Immediately, every woman was on her feet staring straight ahead.

"Prisoner Kowalski, 21060. Your are to report to my office immediately." With that announcement, she strode out the door.

"Oh, M., is this it?" Stefanie took her hand and looked into her face.

"Let's pray that it is, Stef." For a moment, Marissa stared down into those cloud-colored eyes as if she would never see them again.

Reaching into her pocket, Stefanie pulled out a silver cross and pressed it into the palm of Marissa's hand. "Here."

"Where did you—"

"Keep it. I want you to have it. Whenever you look at it, know that you have made a difference here."

Taking the beautifully designed cross, Marissa slipped it into her pocket. "I don't know what to say."

"Don't say anything. If we meet when the war is over, I'll be able to tell you what knowing you has meant to me. Just don't ever forget where you got it."

"Never." Hugging Stefanie tightly, Marissa turned to go and ran into Claudia.

"I wish you the best, Marissa. If there is anything we can ever do for you, don't hesitate to ask."

Marissa smiled up at the gentle giant she had grown to love. "Thank you, my friend. I shall miss you both terribly."

"Be with the one you love, Marissa. It is the only way to survive this madness."

Reaching up to touch Claudia's cheek, Marissa smiled warmly into her face. "And survive I will, Claudia. I swear it. And you?"

Claudia jerked her head in Stefanie's direction. "Keeping that one out of trouble may very well keep me alive."

"Good luck then. I hope to see you on the outside."

Claudia reached out and hugged Marissa tightly. "And if you don't, know that you made our time here easier, and for that, I thank you."

"That means a great deal to me. Take care of Stef. Don't let her become too hard."

"I won't. Now be off, before you anger her."

With that, Marissa headed for the Logiernfuhren's office.

"You wished to see me?"

"Close the door."

Marissa did as she was told and then stood staring straight ahead.

"You are being moved to Barracks C. This has come as a special request from my superiors."

Marissa said nothing, but felt her heart lurch beneath her chest.

"But before you go, I want you to tell me what you can about your friend, Stefanie Sukova."

Marissa felt a pain like a hot poker rip through her stomach. There was no such thing as a free ride, and this woman was going to see to it that she paid for her transfer.

"She is a Czech, Logiernfuhren. From a family of shoe—"

"Enough!" The Logiernfuhren slapped her whip on the table to silence Marissa. "Logiernfuhren Werner relayed to me that she and that moose of a woman are lovers. Is this true?"

Marissa's heart raced. "No, ma'am. I've seen nothing to support that."

Slowly standing up, Logiernfuhren Kohler stood in front of Marissa and stared hard at her. Marissa felt the coldness of her eyes as they surveyed her features. Before Marissa had a chance to flinch, the black whip struck her violently across the cheek, splitting it open like a broken zipper.

"Tell me the truth!"

"I am not lying."

Again, the whip swung across her face, this time sending Marissa crashing against the wall as she threw her hands up to protect her face.

Kohler grunted. "Werner was in such a hurry to leave here she allowed this place to crumble before her very eyes. Well, I will not permit it!" Grabbing Marissa by the throat, she banged her head against the wall. "I don't know what you did to get transferred out of here, but you better believe that it saved your miserable life. As for Sukova, I'm afraid she is not so fortunate."

"They are not lovers."

"Silence!" Stepping away, Kohler raised her whip once more. This time, Marissa looked her square in the face. If she was going to be beaten, she would not shirk away like some dog.

With raised whip, Kohler glared at Marissa as if waiting for her to back down. When Marissa did not, Kohler lowered the whip and tapped it in her palm. "I will find out the truth, you know. And when I do, the three of you will hang. Be gone."

Backing out the door, Marissa was greeted by Fritzi, who wore a ridiculous grin.

"You should have told her the truth, Kowalski."

Feeling the blood ooze down her cheek, Marissa suddenly realized that it was Fritzi who was trying to burn Stefanie and Claudia; Fritzi, who had nothing better to do in this vile place than to play angel to the devil. At that moment, Marissa hated her with every ounce of anger she possessed.

"I did tell her the truth, and you know it."

111

"Do I? All I know is the trouble Sukova brings to me is about to end. I'm sorry that you won't be here to see how it all winds up."

Marissa stopped walking and glowered at Fritzi. For a moment, she had thoughts of attacking her.

"Leave her be, Fritzi."

"Or what?" Fritzi sidled up to Marissa and glowered menacingly at her.

"Or I'll kill you." The words were so foreign and so unnatural sounding coming out of her mouth, Marissa wondered if someone else hadn't said them. She fully expected Fritzi to pummel her right where they stood, but instead, a sick grin trickled across Fritzi's face as she grabbed Marissa's arm and pushed her forward.

"This is my barracks, Kowalski, and my people. Sooner or later, Sukova is going to miss a step, and when she does, I'll be there. You'll have your hands full just trying to survive in Barracks C. I wouldn't worry anymore about Sukova, if I were you."

When they reached the barracks door, Marissa ripped her hand out of Fritzi's grasp and turned to her. "I meant what I said, Fritzi. Leave her alone. Because if I don't get you, someone else will."

Fritzi shook her head; the evil grin still plastered on her face. "Hardly. The women in the warehouse are too weak to lift a needle, let alone have the strength to take on someone my size. No, Kowalski, that's where you're wrong. You women are simply too weak to make such pitiful threats. I'll get Sukova. That much you can be assured of. Now move along. I've got other business to take care of."

"I'm sure you do. And when you're done hurting helpless women, there's a batch of puppies I'm sure need to be kicked as well." Opening the door, Marissa turned to look one last time as the vision of her many nightmares sauntered off into the dark and disappeared among the charcoal shadows, her head back, laughing like some possessed demon.

Chapter Thirty

Holding on to the door, Marissa steadied herself. Her face was throbbing from the bite of Kohler's whip, and her head pounded in time with it. As she entered the barracks, women were preparing for bed.

"Marissa?"

Turning to the voice, Marissa faced Katya. "I am Katya. Elsa's friend."

Marissa only nodded.

"What are you doing here?"

"I have been moved here from the warehouse. Where is Elsa?"

"She worked very hard today. One of the girls could not keep up, so Elsa did both jobs. She's an incredible woman, your Elsa."

"Yes, she is."

"She's in our bunk. It's the fifteenth one on the right."

Before Marissa could start down the aisle, Katya touched her arm. "Would you like to wash those cuts on your face? They look pretty deep."

Lightly running her fingers over her puffy and still bleeding face, Marissa winced as her fingers grazed her split eyebrow.

"I must look hideous."

"I've seen worse. Come. You will scare her to death if you poke your bloody face in hers in the middle of the night." Wringing out a dirty sock, Katya gently wiped the dried blood off Marissa's chin before dabbing at the three-inch gash running perpendicular across her cheek and eyebrow.

"Elsa will be so happy to see you."

Marissa nodded, trying to ignore the pain shooting across her face.

"There. Now you're a bit more presentable."

113

Marissa gazed down at the elfish features of Katya. She reminded her of a mole. "Thank you. You don't mind if I—"

"Be my guest. I'll be up for a while anyway."

Marissa nodded her appreciation and walked down the rows of bunks, counting each one as she went by. Her heart beat heavily against her chest as she approached the fifteenth bunk. After six months, she was finally going to lie in bed with Elsa and hold her in her arms.

Climbing up the bunk, Marissa leaned over and looked into Elsa's face. Her eyes had dark circles underneath them, and her lips were cracked and dry. She was even thinner than the last time Marissa had seen her over a week ago. Alarmingly, Marissa studied the strange cut running along the top of Elsa's forehead.

Tracing her finger over Elsa's nose, Marissa kissed her cheek.

Immediately, Elsa was awake and pushing Marissa away. "Kat, don't! You know—" Stopping in mid-sentence when her eyes focused on Marissa, Elsa threw her arms around Marissa's neck and pulled her on top of her.

"Mari!" she cried, hugging her as tightly as her skinny arms would allow. "What are you doing here?"

"I live here now."

Elsa let her go, and they both sat up.

"What?"

"I had myself moved here."

As Elsa's eyes caught sight of the gashes on Marissa's face, her fingers moved silently and painlessly across them. Her touch seemed to ease the throbbing. "Your face. What happened?"

"It does not matter. The important thing is that we are together."

Elsa's eyebrows knitted together. "What do you mean? How is this so?"

"I asked one of the SS wives to see if she could arrange it. Somehow she fulfilled my request."

Elsa's pupils grew large in the night. "You asked to be moved here?"

"Yes, my love. To be with you."

Elsa shook her head. "You shouldn't have done that."

Marissa was stunned. "What?"

"It was a foolish thing to do, Mari."

"Don't you wish to be with me?" Marissa tried not to sound weak, but her words, her tone, were pleading.

Elsa's frown eased somewhat. "Of course I do, but not here. You were safer in the warehouse. This place is a death trap, Mari. So many die in here every night. You shouldn't have come."

"I don't understand. I thought you would be happy."

Taking Marissa's hand in hers, Elsa kissed it. "I'm happy to see you, but, Mari, women in this barracks are expendable. We are intended to die. Every morning, a dozen bodies are removed; every night, half a dozen collapse and never get back up. You have given up the security and protection from the bitter cold—"

"To be with the woman I love. Don't you think I understand how hard it is to survive here?"

Elsa shook her head sadly. "No, I don't believe you do; otherwise, you would have stayed where your chances of survival were better." Elsa's tone was matter-of-fact, and it surprised Marissa that she was so insistent.

"You are very different now, Elsa."

"As well I should be. Do not get me wrong, Mari. I am very happy to see you, to be with you, but my wish is for you to live. I was happy knowing that you were better off in the warehouse."

Bowing her head, Marissa felt disappointment trickle down her cheek and singe her wound as it dropped in. "I only wanted—"

Taking Marissa's chin and looking into her eyes, Elsa nodded. "I know what you wanted, and I love you even more because of it. I cannot change the fact that you are here."

"Then you're glad I am here?"

Hugging Marissa to her, Elsa shook her head. "Of course I am, silly. I only want what is best for both of us."

"Don't you think being together is what's best?"

Elsa sighed and lay down with Marissa in her arms. "I sure hope so, my love. I just hope you are prepared for the arduous work we face daily."

Snuggling up to Elsa, Marissa did not hear or even feel Katya as she climbed into the bunk.

"I love you so much, Sweetness," Marissa said drowsily.

Laying her free arm across Katya's hips, as she had done every night, Elsa turned and kissed the top of Marissa's forehead.

"I hope you know what you're doing, Mari."

But Marissa was already fast asleep.

Chapter Thirty-One

Elsa was right.

Marissa was not prepared for the biting cold clawing at her skin. The shovel in her hands weighed heavier with every passing second, and there were times when she thought continuing was beyond her.

"Keep working, Mari." Elsa would say. "It is harder to work with boot marks on your back."

Marissa was amazed at how steady Elsa's thin body shovelled the dirt and snow away. Elsa possessed a strength and courage Marissa had not seen in her before and was in awe as Elsa encouraged and prodded the others around them. During the days of hard labor, many looked to Elsa for comfort and support, and she never hesitated offering either.

To Marissa's left, a woman had fallen in the snow, and two guards kicked her until they realized she was already dead. Then they ordered two of the women to pick her body up and move it out of the way.

Turning away, Marissa shuddered. As hard as the work was in the warehouse, it was nothing compared to the daily routine she was now subjected to. With blistered hands and aching back, she trudged back to the barracks when the day's work was complete, often wondering if she hadn't made a terrible mistake.

"I told you this was not the place for you," Elsa said, wrapping Marissa's hands with strips of cloth. No matter how hard she tried, Marissa could not keep from shaking from the cold.

"How . . . how have you managed?"

Elsa grinned. "By looking forward to seeing you again."

Marissa nodded, but sat with her teeth chattering as Katya draped a thin blanket around her shoulders.

"Don't worry, Marissa, the work gets easier once you get used to it. If I can handle a shovel full of snow, anyone can. It's all in your mind."

Elsa looked up from her nursing and saw Yvonne approaching. Since she expressed her desires to Elsa, Katya had steered as far from her as she possibly could. "Here comes Yvonne, Katya. Scoot."

In the week since Marissa had joined her, Elsa had seen the turn the camp was taking in regards to inmate behavior. There were women doing all sorts of sordid things just for a tiny piece of bread. The other day, she saw two women stomping a gypsy for her shoes. And worse yet, one woman was taken away and gassed because she had resorted to cannibalism of her dead bunkmate. There seemed to be no end to the degrading humiliations they were forced to suffer. And in that week's time, Yvonne's hand was heavier and heavier. Elsa wondered if she hadn't lost herself in her Kapo role.

"Elsa, I must speak with you."

Finishing the final bandage, Elsa rose.

"No, Elsa." Marissa said, struggling to get to her feet. "I'll go with you." Placing her hand firmly on Marissa's chest, Elsa shook her head. "It's alright."

"But—"

"But nothing, Mari. I am not afraid of Yvonne."

"You should be."

Elsa shook her head. "Well, I am not. You go rest, and I will be with you when I am finished." Walking over to the window where Yvonne waited, Elsa saw the harsh conditions of the camp reflect in Yvonne's eyes. The price of survival was taking its bite out of Yvonne's spirit as well.

"Marissa must work harder," Yvonne stated flatly.

Elsa nodded. "I know. Give her some time."

"Time is a luxury we do not have. Elsa, today I heard that they are killing twelve thousand of us a day."

The number was too astronomical for Elsa to grasp.

"The selections are happening more frequently now. You must safeguard her if she is to survive."

Elsa nodded and lightly laid a hand on Yvonne's shoulder. She was aware that many were looking on, but she did not care. "And just why do you care, Yvonne? I have seen the frequency of your whip, the heaviness of your hand. Why should you care if another Pole is gassed?"

Yvonne stared at her with saddened eyes. "Before the war, I was biased against so many other Europeans. I was so nationalistic, I believed others to be beneath my kind. Since I've been Kapo, all that has changed. I no longer see the division of nationalities. I see women; women struggling for survival. Your friend, Marissa, is doing just that—struggling."

Elsa opened her mouth to respond, but said nothing. The pain in Yvonne's eyes mirrored the ache in Elsa's spirit.

Yvonne stared out the window. She was silent for a long time before speaking again. "Do you ever look up at the smoke rising from the chimneys and wonder whose soul it is that is twisting its way to freedom?"

"I try not to look. I find it demoralizing."

Yvonne turned to her once more. "I need to know that someone doesn't hate me. I need to know that the changes I've made make a difference." Her eyes were pleading now. "Kapos don't retire, Elsa, they are all killed; if not by the guards, then by the women they beat. Don't you see that I am trapped?"

Elsa leaned against the window and folded her arms across her chest. She was finally grasping what it was that was bothering Yvonne. "It is not my understanding you long for, is it?"

Yvonne said nothing.

"I'm afraid she wants nothing to do with you, Yvonne."

"That's because she has you. If you could only make her see that I could make her life so much easier."

Elsa shook her head sadly. "Yvonne, have you ever considered doing that without exacting a price from her first? Try making her life easier without bargaining for it."

"Do you think—"

119

"I don't know what Katya would do. It seems to me she is open-minded enough about Marissa and me. But who can ever really know?"

Yvonne bowed her head and sighed. "I can't stop thinking about her."

"Try being a little less brutal and see if that changes her heart."

"Do you think there's hope?"

Elsa forced a smile. "Yvonne, hope is what I live on. Without that, we have nothing. Try being a little more gentle. Don't let your Kapo role steal your humanity. You frighten her even though I have tried to explain your case to her. No matter how many of us you save or help, all we really see is your hatred and anger. How do you expect her to come to you when that's all she sees?"

Yvonne shrugged. "I don't know how else to be."

"Try a gentler approach. Don't be afraid to show her a little bit of kindness. You're a woman, Yvonne. Let her see that part of you. Now, I must go before Mari worries too much . . ."

When Elsa got back to the bunk, she found Marissa asleep sitting straight up. Touching her hair and kissing the top of her head, Elsa gently laid her down. Marissa's frame had already shrunken a bit, and the color in her cheeks was a dark ecru. In a week's time, her health was already suffering.

"Oh, Mari," she whispered, softly stroking Marissa's cheek. "What have you done?"

Chapter Thirty-Two

The door banged open, and the guards shouted directions to them in hostile German as they pushed the prisoners out the door. In the confusion, Elsa grabbed Marissa's hand and pulled her to the door.

"What's going on? What's happening?"

"Don't ask, just line up. Something has happened."

Once outside, in the biting cold, Marissa heard talk of escape, of release, of anything other than what it really was. As she stood in line and watched the other barracks fall out into the compound, Marissa saw four ropes hanging above a wooden bench.

"Elsa?"

"Shhh."

From the warehouse came a tall, impeccably dressed man in an SS officer's uniform. Marissa had never seen this officer before. Some whispered it was Hoess, while others said it was Himmler himself. Whoever he was, there was a cruelness, an evil aura surrounding him as he stood and waited for the women in the warehouse to pile out.

As they did, Marissa saw their ashen faces and defeated posture. Many appeared to have been whipped or beaten.

"Stef . . ." Marissa murmured, not seeing Stefanie in the crowd. Instinctively, she took a step forward.

"Mari, don't."

Marissa did not hear her. Scanning the crowd once more, Marissa saw Claudia standing rigidly in the crowd, her face battered and bruised. About four paces away stood Fritzi. For some reason, Marissa could not stop staring at Fritzi's armband.

"Where is Stef?" Marissa asked of no one.

"Mari—" came Elsa's whispered warning.

Then, from behind the warehouse came four prisoners with their hands tied behind their backs. All four displayed battered and bloody faces, and their clothes were blood-soaked and torn. Three of the prisoners were men; the other was Stefanie.

"My God," Marissa whispered as she watched the guards lead them to the makeshift gallows. Marissa stepped forward once more.

"Mari," Elsa growled. "Get back here."

As Stefanie and the three beaten men were forced onto the bench, their nooses were carelessly tossed over their heads. The fight in them had been pummeled away, but they stood proudly erect as the final noose was tightened.

From where she stood, Marissa was in direct line of Stefanie's gaze. Whether Stefanie's one open, gray eye ever saw her, Marissa would never know; the very next moment, the bench was kicked out from under them, and the ropes pulled taut.

In the eerie death silence that followed, Marissa looked over at Claudia, who stood glaring at Fritzi, before returning her gaze to the emotionless SS officer.

"Let that be a lesson to those of you who try to steal from the Reich. You cannot win. The only way to survive is to work. Work makes you free!"

In the next slow-motion moment, Marissa saw movement out of the corner of her eye. It was Claudia.

In three great strides, Claudia had Fritzi by the throat, and in one long arm swing, drove something metallic deep into Fritzi's left eyeball.

Screaming in agony, a long, silver shiv sticking out of her eye, Fritzi dropped to her knees, covering her bloody face with her hands. Before the guards could react, Claudia drove another spike into Fritzi's neck, sending a bright red spurt of blood rising into the air like a fountain. Watching Fritzi writhe on the ground and Claudia standing over her like a statue, Marissa moved ahead a few more steps.

When Claudia turned to Stefanie's dangling and broken body, Marissa watched helplessly as the officer pulled his Luger from his holster and calmly shot Claudia twice in the back.

"No!" Marissa screamed, running over to Claudia.

"Mari, come back!"

But it was too late.

Three steps before she would have reached Claudia's crumpled body, two guards slashed her with their whips, sending her crashing to the ground. Their big, black boots came crashing down on her, and she could feel the welt marks on her back and head rise like yeast.

As Marissa succumbed to the dark unconsciousness rising within her, she opened her eyes once more and peered at the last thing she would see before being beaten insensibly.

Looking out beneath her arms that were protecting her face, Marissa saw one gray-white eye staring up at the heavens.

Chapter Thirty-Three

"Ironically, the only thing that kept the guards from beating Mari to death was Fritzi's death throes. From the depths of her came this low howl that rose in the air like an injured wolf. The officer, who, it turned out, was none other than Himmler himself, raised his Luger and shot her once in the head to silence that wicked tongue forever. Then he ordered her body removed along with Claudia's. As a demoralizer, the Nazis would often let the bodies hang for days to remind us of who was in charge." Elsa shook her head sadly. *"As if we needed reminding."*

Inhaling slowly, Elsa adjusted her mike. "I thought Mari was dead. She might have been had Yvonne not walked over to her, kicked her once, and then violently pulled her to her feet."

"If you do not walk back to the line, Marissa, they will kill you." Yvonne acted angry as she shook Marissa to bring her back to life. "Open your eyes, goddamnit!" she ordered, slapping Marissa once across the face.

Prying one eye open, Marissa stared at her.

"You must walk on your own, or you will be beaten to death. Do you understand me?"

Marissa nodded and straightened her back as far as it would go. Walking with a great deal of pain, Marissa made it back to her place in line and stood as straight and as still as the pain would allow.

"Oh, Mari," Elsa whispered, wanting to reach out and touch her, yet fearful of drawing any more attention to them than they already had. Marissa's cheek had broken open and was dripping off her chin, and there were welt marks on her arms and legs that rose like long, pink leeches.

"Now get back to work and remember what happens to enemies of the Fatherland!" Once in the barracks, Marissa collapsed to the floor.

"Mari!" Elsa cried, kneeling down to her while motioning for Katya to help get her to the bunk.

"She looks bad, Elsa," Katya said, examining Marissa's abrasions and contusions. "If they have hurt her insides, there is nothing we can do for her."

"We must," Elsa stated, hovering over Marissa and wiping blood off her face. "I did not get her back only to lose her now."

When Marissa was cleaned off, Elsa propped her head up and gently stroked her hair. It was so like Marissa to jump up to aid her friends. Another time, another place, it would have been an admirable act. As it was, it could cost her her life.

"They will be coming for us shortly. She must be able to work."

Elsa nodded, still stroking Marissa's hair. "Kat, what are we to do if she cannot work?"

Katya lowered her eyes. "Do your best, Elsa. That is all you can do."

The women waited for hours to go to their work detail, and to Elsa, the delay was a gift from God. Something within the camp must be wrong; otherwise, they would all be working. Whatever it was, Elsa did not care. Every minute gave Marissa more time to come back to life.

"Mari? Can you hear me?"

Marissa nodded slowly.

"Mari, you must be able to work today. If you do not work, they will kill you. Do you understand?"

Swallowing blood, Marissa raised up. "I hurt so much."

"I know you do, but we must get you to your feet. Can you stand?"

Slowly, painfully placing one foot on the floor, then the other, Marissa raised to a sitting position. The room spun angrily about as she reached for Elsa's arm.

"Mari?"

"Help me up," Marissa said, feeling every blow on her back and sides.

Once standing, Marissa shuffled along, using Katya as a crutch. "I . . . think I can manage."

"Maybe so, but work is another story." Helping Marissa back to the bunk, Katya squatted in front of her. "Can you bend over?"

Marissa tried this, but a sharp pain cut through her rib cage and bolted into her temple. "I think my ribs are broken."

Hearing this, Elsa shot down the corridor and quickly returned with more strips of cloth. They looked and smelled as if they had been used as substitutes for toilet paper.

With Katya on one side and Elsa on the other, they wrapped the dirty linen tightly around Marissa's ribs.

"How's that?"

Marissa bent over. "Better. But something inside feels broken."

"You are lucky to be alive, Mari," Elsa said, helping her on with her jacket. "That was a foolish thing you did. You could not have saved her. When will you learn?"

Marissa rubbed her lower back and winced. "I know. I'm sorry."

Kneeling in front of her, Elsa took her hands. "Do not ever be sorry for caring, Mari, but you must learn to be smarter than your emotions. You continue acting emotionally and that will get you hurt or killed. Look at what happened to your friend. Mari, listen to me. Everyone in here is a numb, emotionless creature who eats, sleeps, and works until the day it is safe for us to feel again. You must stop allowing your emotions to rule you, or you'll put us all in danger."

Marissa looked down at Elsa, half expecting to see Stefanie's gray eyes staring at her. Is this what Stefanie tried to tell her? Had Elsa become what Stefanie once was?

"I cannot help it Elsa."

"But you must. Shove your feelings deep down inside you and just concentrate on surviving."

Marissa reached out and touched Elsa's cheek. "Even my love for you?"

Elsa nodded. "Especially that. It takes energy to feel, Mari. We need all of our energy just to live from one hour to the next."

"I . . . I can try. But I don't know how successful I will be."

Kissing Marissa's forehead, Elsa smiled into her eyes. "You will be just fine."

Before Marissa could say another word, the double doors burst open, and two Kapos stood breathless before them.

"Have you heard yet?"

"What?" the women asked, crowding around the Kapos.

"Himmler just had two of his own guards shot."

Elsa stood up and helped Marissa to her feet.

"What for?"

"You'll never believe it, but when they carted Fritzi's body away, Mengele wanted to perform an autopsy on it."

"So!"

"Imagine the look on his face when he discovered that Fritzi was a man!"

For a still moment, no one said a word. No one even moved. And then, ever so softly at first, a chuckle erupted from Marissa. All heads turned to her as she threw her head back and roared through the pain in her ribs.

"Mari? What is it?"

The women in the barracks now crowded around Marissa.

"That explains so much," Marissa said, sitting on the bunk. "The woman who was hanged, Stefanie Sukova, was a dear friend of mine. She must have known about Fritzi's secret because she always spoke to her, him, whatever, as if she was holding something over his head."

Elsa sat next to Marissa. "How could this have happened?"

"So many of the SS are homosexual," the Kapo answered. "We heard that Himmler shot the two guards who placed Fritzi in the women's compound in exchange

127

for . . . well . . . certain favors. Apparently, he was quite . . . useful to many of the guards as well. If you know what I mean."

Marissa nodded. It all made sense now. Somehow, probably while she was thieving in the night, Stefanie uncovered Fritzi's secret and used it against him. After failing at accusing her of being a lesbian, Fritzi must have found other alternatives to use against Stefanie. For as long as Stef was alive, Fritzi would risk getting caught.

"Anyway, that's why the delay." Scooting out the door, the two Kapos vanished.

"That was quite a place you came from," Katya said, shaking her head.

"And they were quite a duo." Walking away from the crowd, Marissa reached into her pocket and pulled out the cross Stefanie had given to her. From the pit of her stomach, an emptiness spread throughout her entire being. She hadn't just lost two friends; she had experienced the searing pain that was the foundation of the concentration camp experience—the slow, agonizing demoralization and realization that one was in control of nothing.

Looking out the window and squeezing the cross into her palm, Marissa sighed. She didn't think it possible to feel the emptiness she was feeling now. Two fine women were lost to the world, and the realization struck her hard and deep. Marissa wanted to cry for the loss, but remembered Elsa's words. There would be plenty of time to cry later. For now, she would live, and she would carry on with the promise Stef made to herself.

"You're free now, Stef," she whispered, staring at the cross. "Free."

Chapter Thirty-Four

"The internal injuries that Marissa suffered in the winter of 1944 deteriorated her health considerably. Whether she was experiencing kidney failure or the infection of another organ, we did not know. What we did know was that it was becoming exceedingly difficult to get her up in the morning, and she was barely able to lift half a shovel of snow. Marissa was dangerously close to selection." Elsa reached behind her and touched Marissa's hand.

"Seeing Stefanie and Claudia killed took more life out of Marissa than we knew. It was as if she didn't believe she could make it anymore. Add to that her internal injuries, and I knew she was steps away from the next selection."

One night, when Marissa had fallen asleep, Katya rolled over close to Elsa.

"She's dying, Elsa. You know that, don't you?"

Elsa stared into the darkness and said nothing. She saw it, but did not want to believe it.

"Without some kind of medication, she'll die. The beating is taking its toll on her, Elsa. I think she might have ruptured something inside."

Elsa stroked Marissa's hair as she slept. "What would you have me do, Kat? You think I don't notice how little she works or how haunting she has become? I've seen others who are in better health than Marissa never wake up. I go to sleep every night with the fear that the same will happen to her. I'm scared that I'm going to wake up to find her dead. I've given her extra clothing; she eats half my ration; I don't know what more I can do."

Katya reached across Marissa and patted Elsa's hand. "I am sorry if I offended you. I see how you suffer over her, and I just think there must be something we can do."

"We can just try to keep her moving, Katya. I don't know what else to do."

The next morning, Elsa awoke with Marissa still in her arms, but Katya was not in bed.

"Mari, we must get up."

Raising her head slightly, Marissa looked at Elsa through two glassy orbs. The light that had always reflected from her emerald eyes was a mere flicker now as her sickness colored the whites of her eyes a pale yellow. Her breathing was raspy, and she rattled like she had dried leaves in her lungs.

"Leave me, Sweetness. I cannot go on."

Grabbing Marissa and yanking her to her feet, Elsa shook her. "You must! You must and you will! Damn you, Marissa Kowalski, don't you dare give up on me!"

Marissa coughed up a wad of phlegm. "If I go today, Elsa, they will beat me, and I cannot survive another beating."

"You will not live if you stay here."

Marissa's eyes cast down at the dirty floor. "I came here to keep you alive, and now . . . now I am the burden."

Throwing her arms around Marissa's neck, Elsa pleaded. "No, Mari, don't say that. A burden would be having to live without you. Don't make me do that. Don't make me live alone for the rest of my life. I need you. You're all I have left."

Feeling the pain in her lower back and ribs every time she inhaled, Marissa nodded. "I will try."

Taking Marissa's yellowing face in her hands, Elsa gently kissed her. "That's all any of us are doing, Mari—trying. You must wake up every morning wanting to live."

Coughing again, Marissa nodded. "I'll do my best."

Taking Marissa's tender frame in hers, Elsa held her for a long moment before line up.

"I love you, Mari. I need you to live."

"Then I will do that, Sweetness. I will do that."

Chapter Thirty-Five

Marissa and Elsa stood together at the podium holding hands. The image of the two survivors indelibly imprinted on the minds of the young, female audience would serve as a reminder of the accomplishments that could be made when love was the cement of the spirit. That love was evident now.

Clearing her throat, Elsa spoke. "It was mid-December of 1944 when Mari became so ill we had to practically carry her to the compound every morning. The Nazis had stepped up Endlosung or the 'Final Solution' because it was becoming quite clear they were losing the war. The only war they could concentrate on winning was the war against the Jews and other 'undesirables.' Day and night, the ovens were stoked with human fuel as the selection process became an hourly occurrence. There was talk and evidence that the Russians would soon be upon us, but the Nazis paid little heed. Instead, they sped up the mass murder machines and continued stuffing as many people into the shower chambers as they could."

Elsa paused here to sip some water; the strain on her face showing the pain of the images forever locked in her memory. "Historical estimates concur with the rumors Yvonne had heard: twelve thousand people a day were destroyed at Auschwitz alone. I'm no historian, but I say that figure is too low. But, regardless, we knew that they were killing thousands of us, and keeping Mari from being selected became my major concern.

"Prior to inspection, we would pinch Mari's cheeks, wipe out her eyes, and force her to stand tall. I would hold my breath every time the guards would come near her. It was almost more than I could bare."

For the first two weeks in December, Elsa awoke with only Marissa in the bed. She had said nothing to Katya, who was an early riser anyway, but she was beginning to worry about the little woman's strange disappearances.

Then, one morning, she discovered just where Katya had been going. As Elsa climbed out of the bunk, she found Katya waiting for her in the darkness. "Katya, where have you been?"

Holding out her hand, Katya opened it to reveal four tiny, white pills. "It's penicillin."

Elsa stared down at the tiny hand in disbelief. "How did you . . ." Kneeling in front of Katya, Elsa closed her hand around Katya's. "You didn't."

Katya's blue eyes blinked several times before she spoke. "I had to. She'll die if we don't stop the infection. She said she had connections at the hospital. I . . ."

Taking Katya into her arms, Elsa squeezed her. "Oh, Katya."

Pulling away, Kat held her hand out again and dropped the pills into Elsa's hand.

"Are you sure these are penicillin? They could be something else."

Katya shrugged. "We must trust that it is."

The words made Elsa wince. "Trust?" It was an odd notion. No one trusted the Kapos.

Katya bowed her head. "Yvonne said she saw the bottle herself. She does not wish Marissa harm, Elsa. I . . . I trust her."

Elsa, still squatting, dropped the pills into her pocket and held Katya's hands in hers. "You trust a woman who exchanges sexual favors for medication?"

Katya bit her lip and looked down into Elsa's face. "It was I who initiated this, Elsa. It was only yesterday that I asked her for the pills."

"Kat, you didn't need to . . . you shouldn't have. How long have you been sleeping with her?"

"Almost two weeks."

Elsa was stunned. "Two weeks. Oh, Katya, you did all of this for the pills?"

Katya nodded. "She is the only one who can help."

Pulling Katya to her, Elsa hugged her tightly. "You are an incredible friend, my little Katya. I only wish you did not have to make such a sacrifice."

Backing away, Katya shook her head. "It is not so bad as you think, Elsa. She is very gentle with me. And when

I asked her to see if she could get some medication for Marissa, she did not hesitate."

"Then she is not the monster you thought her to be?"

"Not at all. She . . ." Katya blushed crimson. "She is extremely tender."

Elsa, for the first time in almost a year, felt a sprout of emotion push its way through her hardened exterior. "Perhaps because she loves you?"

Katya shrugged. "I don't really know. She touches me like one who does."

"I don't know what to say to thank you."

"You saved my life once, Elsa. I know that Marissa is as much your life as your own heart is. I am not about to lose either of you."

"But I did not have to sleep with anyone—"

Katya waved her off. "It's not like you think it is. She doesn't ravage me, Elsa. Some nights we just talk, some we cuddle away from the cold, and others . . . she . . . well . . . wants to be with me."

Elsa said nothing, only took each of Katya's hands and kissed them. "She is a very lucky woman."

Katya blushed a deeper red. "Oh, I don't know about that. I am . . . very clumsy. You would think I did not know much about a woman's body."

This brought a smile to Elsa's face. "Oh, little Katya, I do love you so." Hugging Katya tightly, Elsa rose. "You are truly a good friend."

Grabbing Elsa's wrist, Katya pulled her closer. "But I'm afraid—"

"That she will want more of you?"

Katya shook her head. "No. That . . . I am not a very good lover. Perhaps . . .," Katya said, lowering her voice, "you could tell me more about . . . well . . . you know . . . what to do?"

Walking with Katya back to the bunk, Elsa nodded. "You wish to please her?"

"I wish to . . . not be such a klutz."

Elsa grinned to herself. "I see. Then I will tell you what I know so you can . . . not be such a klutz."

Smiling, Katya nodded. "Thank you."
"No, my Katya. Thank you."

Chapter Thirty-Six

"The medication helped save Marissa's life," Elsa explained after a brief intermission. "But our greatest fear remained vivid as the Nazis were shoving and packing the showers so tightly; people were gassed standing up. And although the penicillin stymied the infection running through her body, it did nothing to ease her pain or heal the wounds of her heart."

Marissa nodded and added, "Parts of me were dying, and I could not find the will I'd had in the beginning. Stef's and Claudia's deaths affected me more than I realized because of all the women I had met, I expected them to survive. And then, when I became sick, so much energy was expended in keeping my physical being healthy that I did not have the energy to focus on my spirit, which was breaking off into tiny pieces every day."

One morning, Katya crawled into bed in the early hours. Placing her hand on Marissa's forehead as she did every time she got in bed, she turned to wake Elsa up.

"Her fever is up."

Elsa felt Marissa's head and cringed. "We have no more medicine."

Instantly, Katya jumped off the bunk and returned with snow wrapped in a dirty shirt. "Put this on her forehead."

Elsa did so and held Marissa close to her. "I don't know how she sleeps when she is burning up."

Katya snuggled up to Elsa and laid her head on her shoulder.

"Well, Katya, how did it go?"

Katya squirmed. "I think I was better. She seemed pleased."

Holding Marissa in her right arm and Katya in her left, Elsa pulled both closer. "You needn't sleep with her anymore, Katya. The medication seems not to affect Mari as well as it once did."

Katya did not respond.

"Katya? Did you hear me?"

"Yes."

"Well?"

"Well . . . I . . ."

Elsa looked down at Katya. She could see the outline of her face in the cold darkness. "You care for her, don't you?"

Katya turned her face away. "If I said I did, would you think less of me?"

"Of course not. But I would tell you I am a bit surprised."

"Elsa, Yvonne is very good to me. When we are together, she holds me and caresses me, and sometimes she hums a tune in my ear. If I didn't know better, I would think she was in love with me."

"And you?"

Katya shrugged. "I don't think I would know how to feel it for a woman."

Elsa lightly pressed her lips against Katya's cheek. "Marissa once told me that love has no gender. If you feel it, it's love."

Before Katya could reply, Marissa mumbled and thrashed around in her heated sleep.

"Elsa?" Marissa groaned.

"I'm right here, honey."

Opening her eyes, Marissa squinted, trying to focus in the dark. "I'm so hot."

In the freezing winter at Auschwitz, Marissa Kowalski was probably the only inmate out of one hundred thousand to ever utter those words.

"You'll be okay," Elsa purred, placing the melting snow-rag back on Marissa's face.

"Will I? I feel so weak. Elsa, you must go on without me. You must save your strength." Marissa's eyes fluttered before closing. "Josef and your Papa . . . they need you."

Kissing Marissa's hot cheek as it lowered back to her shoulder, Elsa turned and looked at Katya, who was starting down the bunk.

"Where are you going?"

"You know where. There must be something she can do."

"Katya, don't. It's too late."

"No, Elsa, it is never too late."

Chapter Thirty-Seven

The next morning, they were awakened before dawn for yet another selection. All night long, bombs and rifle shots could be heard in the distance, and many of the women began mumbling about this being the day of freedom. Instead, they were greeted by the death masks of the guards and Kapos whose job it was to escort prisoners to the showers.

"Elsa! A selection! Get Marissa up!"

But Marissa barely moved. Her entire body was covered with sweat, and her head rolled from side to side when Elsa shook her.

"Damnit, Mari, please wake up!" Slapping Marissa across the face, Elsa helplessly glanced up at the incoming death squad. "Mari, please, I am begging you to open your eyes and get up."

Slowly, ever so slowly, one eye opened, followed by the other. "I am so thirsty. Can I have some water?"

"Marissa, you must get up, or they will kill you. Please, get up for me."

Marissa looked at Elsa as if she did not know her, so raging was the fever within. Trying to focus on the face swimming before hers, Marissa nodded. "Up."

"Remember Tory's Tuesday?" Marissa asked. Her appearance, her heaviness of tongue and slow movements, reminded Elsa of a drunk woman.

"Marissa, you must be able to stand here on your own. Can you do that for me?"

Nodding, Marissa backed slowly away. Her head felt like her hair was on fire.

"Like this?"

Elsa nodded and shot a fearful glance at Katya.

"Sweetness?"

"Yes, my love?"

"I don't think I can make it today."

"You will, just like you have every day."

Marissa nodded and wiped the sweat off of her top lip with the back of her hand. "Do you know . . .," she said, wavering back and forth until Katya put a hand out to steady her. "Do you know how very much I love you?"

Elsa nodded. "Yes, I do." Realizing that Marissa's delirium could no longer be hidden, Elsa felt the panic rising in her.

"Good. And do you know—"

"Marissa, not now. Please, honey, do not say another word."

Suddenly, the doors bashed open and the death squad walked in. Looking down at the clipboard, the officer in charge was walking down an aisle, flicking a wrist at certain, unfortunate prisoners.

"This one, this one, that one," she said, sometimes reading the numbers on their arms, and other times just choosing them at random.

"Katya?"

"Hush, Marissa."

"Katya, I cannot stand here any longer," Marissa whispered out of the corner of her mouth.

"This one, this one. Hmmm, this one."

"You must, Marissa," Katya whispered back.

"This one, this one, hell, we should have just bombed this entire barracks. This one."

"Elsa?"

"Shhh."

"Elsa, I love you." With that, Marissa crumpled to the floor in a heap.

"No!" Diving to the floor, Elsa took Marissa in her arms. "Don't you dare leave me alone, Marissa Kowalski! You promised! You promised me—"

Crack went the whip across Elsa's back.

Immediately, Katya pulled Elsa away from Marissa. "Elsa, they'll take you, too. She would want you to live!"

"No!" Elsa cried, feeling herself restrained by hands stronger and larger than Kat's. Turning around, she was face to face with Yvonne.

"Let her go, Elsa," Yvonne said gently. "You cannot help her now. You did everything you could."

"No."

The guard turned and struck Elsa across the face. "Silence!" Glaring at Elsa, who would not look anywhere else, except at Marissa's crumpled body, the guard decided to pass her over.

"Ahh, here we come to Mengele's special request," the officer remarked, looking down at Katya.

Upon hearing his name, Katya let out a screech. The sound stirred something in Marissa, who groaned and rolled over on her side.

"Doktor Mengele is not happy that a dwarf has escaped his probing. He will be pleased to have you under his microscope."

Suddenly, Yvonne was standing next to Katya. "No. Take me instead. Check my papers, and you will see that I have a twin brother on the other side of camp."

The officer tapped the whip in her hand while considering. In the tense seconds that elapsed like an eclipse, Marissa managed to wobble to her feet.

"Perhaps the good Doktor would be twice as happy with two, eh?" Turning to her assistants, the officer spat out, "Set those two aside for special handling."

Pushing Katya over to Yvonne, the officer motioned over at Marissa. "You two will bring her with you."

Elsa made a slight movement toward the three women, but Yvonne straight armed her away.

"Don't. Live for us, Elsa. It's the best you can do." Putting her arm around Marissa, who slowly reached for Elsa, Yvonne pulled her away. "Come, Marissa, before they take her as well."

"I love you, Mari," Elsa shouted as they made their way to the door. "I will love you forever."

Trying to focus on the tear-stained face across the barracks, Marissa nodded. "I love you, too, Sweetness. See you Tuesday at Tory's." And with that, they followed the large group heading out the door.

Chapter Thirty-Eight

"How are you feeling?" Yvonne asked, helping Marissa along.

"Does it matter? Soon, I won't be feeling at all." Marissa barely noticed the crowd of women moving around her, awaiting a similar fate.

"Are you afraid?" Katya asked, pulling Marissa closer to her.

Marissa shook her head. "No. It's odd. I am not relieved and I am not frightened. I don't really know what I feel. Are you?"

Katya nodded. "I do not want to be dissected like some laboratory animal. I would rather die quickly. I would rather die with you." Her last sentence was directed toward Yvonne.

"I would wish that none of us had to die like this."

Katya cocked her head to the side and gazed up at Yvonne. "Why did you do that? Why did you offer yourself?"

Their arms around Marissa's waist, Katya and Yvonne half carried, half supported, Marissa. Rattling as she inhaled, Marissa answered before Yvonne could speak.

"Because she loves you, Kat. Can't you see that?"

Katya looked up at Marissa's face. "Is that your delirium speaking?"

Marissa shook her head. "No. I believe it is the truth. And I think you know it, too."

Suddenly, sounds of the raging war around them exploded on the grounds just outside the gates, showering rocks and snow onto the compound.

"The Bolsheviks!" Yvonne cried, pointing to the smoke on the crest of a hill.

"They've been here for days, Yvonne. They're not going to save us."

Marissa squinted to see. "Maybe not us, but perhaps Elsa and the others." Laboring to breathe, Marissa leaned against Yvonne. "God, how I want her to live."

The rat-tat-tatting of machine gun fire could be heard from the woods north of where they stood.

"They're awfully close," Yvonne noted, eyeing the movement of troops over the hill's peak.

"Look at the guards in the compound. They're panicking."

A harried guard ran over to the officer in charge and shouted at her to get these inmates to the showers immediately. A few more rushed words passed between them before the guard turned and pointed at Yvonne and Katya.

"But these two are for the Doktor."

"Mengele left camp hours ago. Now do as I told you!"

The officer turned to the crowd and ordered them to march down the road.

"What is going on?" Katya wondered aloud.

Marissa watched anxiously as Nazis hopped in jeeps, ran around the compound, and escorted SS and other high-ranking officials out of the camp. Outside of the gates, guns and grenades exploded into the brittle air.

Turning down the dirt and gravel road leading to the waterless showers, the trio looked carefully at one another. Overhead, bombs were popping in the air, bullets were ripping through trees, and Nazis everywhere were scrambling around like black ants running crazily when the food they are preying upon is taken away.

"The Nazis are running scared," Yvonne said, motioning to a truckload of guards leaving the compound. "The Red Army must be very close to taking this area."

As they were shoved closer and closer to the showers, Marissa straightened up and tried to walk on her own. Looking at the herd of humans walking down the path, Marissa estimated several hundred prisoners were slated to inhale the poisonous gasses.

"We can't go in. Not yet. Not if the camp is being liberated. Yvonne?" Marissa turned to her and squeezed her hand.

"It's better than being tortured, Mari," Katya replied. "The Russians may liberate the camp, but not before we see the inside of the showers."

"Wait!" Yvonne commanded, turning back to look at the chaotic compound.

As Marissa's eyes travelled the same route to see what Yvonne was looking at, she realized she was staring at the tall towers guarding the camp. Only this time, instead of their weapons being trained on the prisoners within the camp, several of the machine gunners were busy firing their guns at targets outside of camp.

"The Bolsheviks must be right here," Yvonne said, still staring at the towers. "Who else would they be shooting at?"

Marissa turned and looked at Katya. They were only a hundred meters away from the showers now. Death waited for them with open arms, and like so many thousands before them, they were almost willing to embrace it.

Almost.

"Marissa, can you run?" Yvonne asked, still looking back at the camp.

Marissa frowned. "I'm not even sure I can walk."

Yvonne grabbed Marissa's neck and brought her face to within inches of Marissa's. "You promised her, Marissa. You owe it to both of you to try."

"Try what? What are you talking about?"

Yvonne eyed the frightened guard walking several paces behind them. "Our only chance is to make a break for the woods."

Katya nodded, her eyes suddenly lighting up. "If the Russians are here, they my liberate the camp within a few hours or a few days. We don't have time to find out which. What do you say, Mari? A bullet in the back or gas up the nose?"

Marissa thought of Elsa's face when she walked into the bakery every morning. She thought about their long walks in the summer and their talks at Tory's. She thought about poor Josef and Elsa's Papa. She thought about Stefanie's one gray eye staring into the heavens and Claudia's crumpled body on the ground. She did not have to think long. "I'll run if I have to do it on my hands."

Yvonne grabbed Katya's and Marissa's hands. "Good. Then here's what we must do."

Chapter Thirty-Nine

Elsa looked into the crowd of intense faces. Most of the young audience were literally on the edge of their seats. "Once the three of them were taken away, I just stood there, staring out at the cold dawn. It was odd. I felt nothing; no sorrow, no pain, nothing. I think it was so unreal to me that I did not believe it was actually happening. To have the one whom you love more than life itself be stripped away was not something I was emotionally equipped to handle. So I just stood and waited. What I waited for, I do not know." Elsa looked over her shoulder at Marissa. The pain and sorrow of that frightening moment oozed between them even now as the memory of her loss hung tangibly in the air.

"And then I heard the bombs and machine gun fire, and I watched the Nazis clambering around trying to defend themselves from real soldiers. It was then that I ran to the window to see if I could see my love walking toward the showers. It was incredible to me that, even as they were being attacked, the mindless Nazi killing machine continued packing bodies into the ovens. In their fear of being caught at what we now call genocide, they began shooting prisoners, moving whole barracks to be shot into mass burials, and trying to cover up years of atrocities." Here, Elsa ceased as the corners of her mouth quivered.

Marissa laid her hand on her shoulder and smiled tenderly into her face. "Go on."

"I realized there was a ray of hope that Marissa, Katya, and Yvonne might not be gassed if only the Russians arrived in time. To my knees I fell to offer a prayer to a God I had long since abandoned. It was such a tiny fragment of hope, but I held onto it with all my heart. Because I knew if there was a way to survive Yvonne would find it."

Marissa leaned over and said softly into the mike, "And find it, she did."

As the machine gun and rifle explosions blasted nearer, Yvonne, Katya, and Marissa nodded to each other. If they were going to die, it would not be standing like cattle in the slaughterhouse.

"Run!"

As Marissa and Katya broke from the crowd, Yvonne rushed the guard, pushed him to the ground, and crushed his head with a rock before he could fire a single round. Grabbing his rifle, she fired a few rounds in the direction of the other guards, both of which dropped heavily to the ground like two marionette puppets whose strings had just been cut.

"Run, Katya! Stay with Mari!" Swinging the rifle around, Yvonne squeezed the trigger three more times, killing a young officer who was bringing up the rear.

"All of you, run! The Russians are here! Run for your lives!"

The other prisoners looked at each other and at Yvonne with confusion. It was as if she had interrupted the moment they had come to embrace.

"Run, damnit!"

While only a quarter of the prisoners fled for the woods, it was enough to create added chaos for the guards who must have thought they were being attacked by the Russian army.

As the hundred or so prisoners scattered, Yvonne knelt down, took aim, and fired off seven rounds before finally hitting the machine gunner who had started firing at the fleeing crowd.

"Come on, Yvonne!" Katya cried, waving at her from the edge of the woods.

Several guards came running from the building, but Yvonne gunned them down as well before scurrying past prisoners struggling up the short embankment.

"Where's Mari?" Yvonne asked, grabbing Katya's hand and pulling herself up.

"I told her to keep running, that we'd find her. I don't think she'll get very far."

A spray of bullets riddled the ground at her feet.

"Keep moving!"

Running through the woods, tree branches slicing their faces and arms, Yvonne and Katya could hear the resounding popping of guns and the sick thud of flesh as sightless bullets hit their targets. Before them, half a dozen people lay dead or dying from a gunshot wound to the back. Still more fell in front of them as the Nazi guards fired at random into the woods.

"There's Mari!" Katya shouted, pointing to Marissa, who wobbled through the woods like a drunkard.

Straining to put one foot in front of the other, her head pounding, lungs heaving and whistling, face bleeding from being whipped by the branches, Marissa was running faster than anyone else in the woods.

"Where . . . to?" Marissa wheezed, arms and legs still churning when Yvonne and Katya caught up to her.

"Just keep running. Where . . . ever that takes us."

The bark of the trees around them cracked and thudded as bullets crashed into them. All around them, the sounds of bullets could be heard tearing through leaves, digging up snow and dirt, and, all too often, lodging in bodies.

"Keep running!" Yvonne ordered. On a single pivot, Yvonne squatted, aimed the heavy rifle, and blew a hole out the back of a guard who had pursued them into the woods. As she swung the rifle around to shoot his compatriot, a bullet smashed through her left shoulder, knocking her back against a tree.

In that instant, Katya had glanced back to see where Yvonne was and watched in horror as a bullet exploded out of her back.

"No!" Katya cried, turning back. As Katya started to run to her, Marissa grabbed her arm.

"Leave her, Kat."

"No! She saved our lives, Marissa. I will not turn my back on her now." Ripping her arm out of Marissa's grasp, Katya ran back to Yvonne.

Marissa remembered Yvonne picking her up after her brutal beating and telling her she had to walk back to line on her own, or they would kill her. She, too, had been saved by Yvonne's courage. Turning back, Marissa caught up with Katya and Yvonne.

"She's alive," Katya said as bullets pinged and danced all around them.

"Get down, Katya," Yvonne ordered, coughing.

"Can you run?" Marissa asked as snow behind her kicked up.

Yvonne shook her head. "Not unless we take out . . . the guard following us." Yvonne groped for the rifle. "He'll kill us all if we don't."

"I'll do it." Grabbing the gun, Katya steadied it and fired once, but her aim was way off.

"Put it on your shoulder Katya and hold steady. When I say hold, I want you to hold your breath." Blood was oozing down Yvonne's back, and Marissa wondered how long it would be before she passed out.

"Hold."

The four cracks from the rifle instantly silenced the pinging bullets.

"Got him!" Katya cried, clapping her hands. But Yvonne merely sank back against the tree.

Bending down to look at her wounds, Katya laid the rifle next to her. "You're bleeding pretty badly."

"Here." Taking her striped jacket off, Marissa unwound the linen from her ribs and wrapped Yvonne's bleeding shoulder. "It looks like the bullet came right out. That's good."

Yvonne nodded, her eyelids getting heavy.

"Where on earth did you learn to shoot like that?" Katya asked, helping her to her feet.

"My father was a big hunter. I had no brothers, and my sister was too prissy to go, so he always took me. I first learned how to shoot with the rifle on his shoulder like we just did."

Katya stared at her. "But you said you were a twin and that your brother was—"

"I lied."

Moving through the woods slowly, they met other prisoners who were turning back to the camp. Afraid of exposure, afraid of living, these tormented souls sought the peace of death rather than the uncertainty of life.

"I do not know how much farther I can go," Yvonne said as they stepped over a snow-covered log. They were a good half-mile from the camp now. "You must leave me and save yourselves."

"No." Katya stated firmly as she brushed the snow off the log to sit down.

Painfully, Yvonne turned and took Katya's hands in hers. "Yes, Katya, you must. Soon, I will lose consciousness, and you cannot carry me. Don't be foolish. Save yourselves."

Katya looked at Marissa, who felt as if her fiery head would explode any minute.

"Mari?"

Marissa stared at the tiny woman whose eyes pleaded with her. She looked over at the tall, bleeding giant who had saved their lives more than once. There was no question of what to do.

"You stay here with Yvonne. If she goes into shock, your body heat will help keep her warm. I'll go see if I can find a village or something. There must be someone around here sympathetic to us."

"How will you know where we are?"

Marissa looked up at the sun hiding behind a cloud. "If I'm not back by the time the sun reaches those trees, you must find someplace to go for the night, or you will die of exposure."

Katya nodded. "Before we leave here, I will shoot the rifle three times in case you are near or are lost."

Yvonne reached for the rifle and disengaged a bayonet connected to the barrel. "Perhaps . . . you can mark . . . your way with this."

Taking the bayonet from Yvonne, Marissa nodded and looked underneath the log they were sitting on. "You're better off under here in case they come along."

In a few minutes, they dug a shallow cave, lowered Yvonne into it, and scrounged up dead branches to cover the opening.

"Perfect," Katya said, examining their work. Putting her hand on Marissa's shoulder, Katya squeezed it. "Perhaps I should go."

149

Marissa fought off the pain kicking her lower back. "Perhaps. But answer me this. Do you love her?"

Katya's reply was a single nod.

"I ask because if our positions were reversed, if it was Elsa with a bullet hole in her back, you could not pry me away from her."

Katya nodded again.

"Then, do you love her, Kat?"

"Yes."

"Would you rather stay with her?"

"Yes, Mari. Besides, I have the worst sense of direction. If I got lost, if something happened to her because I couldn't find my way back, I would never forgive myself."

Marissa touched the top of Katya's head. "Say no more."

"But how are you feeling?"

"My head is pounding, and my lungs are about to burst, but this feels better than anything I've ever felt in my life. I want to go. You stay and take care of Yvonne and know you're doing the right thing." Marissa bent down and hugged her. "You've saved my life twice Katya. If anything should happen and I don't come back . . . know that I think you are the bravest woman I have ever met."

"You'll come back, Mari. You must."

As the two women looked into each other's face, words and emotions flowed between them like a river of knowledge. Brought together by the cruelest of fates, neither were ready or willing to let go of the friendship they had sewn together from fragments of lost emotions. If they never saw each other again, each would remain a vivid and warm memory for the other.

"Go now. We mustn't waste any time." Katya stood on her tiptoes and kissed Marissa's cheek. "Godspeed, Mari, and come back to us."

Chapter Forty

"Everything and everybody in camp was insane. The Nazis were burning things, burying gold, unburying other treasures, running here and there, and threatening prisoners and each other. When the Red Army burst through the gates, they stood speechless and motionless as the thousands of living corpses stared back at them through vacant eyes. So many did not know enough to be happy that freedom had come; few believed that it truly had. Hope realized is more than a miracle, and miracles were not something we believed in."

Upon viewing the foul and fetid corpses lying behind the barracks, several broad-shouldered soldiers heaved at the sight of emaciated bodies piled like firewood awaiting their turn for the ovens. Other soldiers knelt down on the soil and offered their tears to the skeletal remains of those who stood by waiting their fate.

It was a moment in time when no one moved; not soldiers or prisoners of war. Like a framed painting needing to be interpreted, seconds ticked by with no sounds, no movement, no life. It was as if the powerful death machine grinded to a halt and left the universe in utter silence.

And then, as the shock of seeing the living skeletons wore down, the soldiers looked to each other for some sort of reassuring signal that what they were seeing was, in fact, reality.

In the strange Russian language, they spoke slowly as if unsure of what to do next. Not even the battle-worn officers knew how to react to the gruesome sights before them. No one seemed to know what to do.

Except Elsa.

Realizing that they were now free, understanding that the Russians had, indeed, driven the Nazis out, she ran past the green-clad soldiers and down the trail toward the showers. Along the way, she ran into several guards with their hands laced together over their helmets. Behind them stood Russian soldiers with rifles held at their backs.

"Where are you going?" A young Russian officer asked in Slavic-accented German.

"The showers!" Elsa said. "Please, open the showers. My . . . friend might be in there. Please!"

The soldier looked at his friend, puzzled. "Showers?"

"Please, open the doors and let me see."

"The showers are locked?"

Elsa grabbed his arm and impatiently pulled him toward the building. "I am begging you, please help me open those doors!"

"Alright, alright," he said, turning to the other soldier and barking out a command before grabbing one of the Nazi guards and ordering him to open the doors.

The frightened guard shook as he did what he was told, yet no one, not even the Russian soldiers, were prepared for the sight before them.

Inside one large room stood dozens upon dozens of dead people. Urine, feces, blood, and other bodily fluids dripped slowly down their legs. Some had no eyeballs, some had claw marks on their faces, and all were naked, slightly blue, and very dead.

"Do not permit anyone in here," the officer ordered, gagging back the bile in his throat.

The other Russian officer bent over and vomited in the bushes just outside the showers. "My God," he uttered, staring at the morbid scene before him.

"My friend—" Elsa pleaded, trying to see inside the showers.

The officer turned to Elsa as if forgetting she was the one who asked to have the showers opened.

"I thought you said showers."

Elsa shook her head. "Gas showers, sir. When will you let me in?"

The soldiers were so overwhelmed at the task ahead of them that it was several hours before the bodies were removed. No one was prepared for the massive body count or sickness pervading the camp. None of the officers in charge seemed to know where to begin. The only thing they knew for sure was that the living had priority over the dead. Even that lived up to the status quo of Auschwitz.

Hours later, Elsa stood by the showers and waited for the soldiers to start loading the bodies onto a long, wooden cart. Everywhere she turned, the long carts were piled high with bodies.

"Well?" asked the soldier who had thrown up in the bushes.

"She isn't here. I don't understand it."

Gently taking Elsa's arm, the soldier moved her away from the cart. "I heard there was a small group that ran into the woods when we approached. Perhaps she was with them."

Elsa looked at the clean-shaven face of the soldier. He was just a boy. "Thank you for your kindness." Looking out at the woods, Elsa saw footprints running up the embankment. Perhaps Marissa had been one of those who escaped, although she could not see how Marissa could walk, let alone climb an embankment. But her Mari was a strong-willed woman, and she had Yvonne and Katya with her. As long as there was a thread of hope, Elsa would believe Marissa was alive.

Walking over to the embankment, Elsa looked down at the snow-covered ground and the footprints formed neatly in it. Maybe the three of them were able to escape during the confusion of the raid. Maybe they were able to get away before the others were stuffed into the showers. Maybe . . .

Out of the corner of her eye, something glistened beneath the bright rays of the sun. Bending over, Elsa stared at the silver cross Marissa had shown her the night after Stefanie was killed. Slowly reaching for it as if touching it would make it disappear, Elsa picked it up and clutched it to her breast.

"Oh, Mari. Tell me this means you escaped. Tell me this cross fell from your pocket as you fled from death." Looking down at the cross, Elsa held it firmly in her palm. The chain, like her love for Marissa, was unbroken. If Marissa was alive, she would find her. If it took the rest of her life, she would search until she knew the truth about what happened to Marissa Kowalski; she would never rest until she knew Marissa was alive. And if she wasn't, she was sure she would feel it. And Elsa did not feel it.

Chapter Forty-One

Marissa's head was pounding so much it hurt to take a step. Pushing through the snowy thicket, Marissa was determined to find a safe haven for the three of them. After all, they were still in her country, and she was sure she could find someone who would want to help them.

Twice during her escape through the woods, Marissa passed prisoners stumbling in the snow as well. Looking up at the sun, Marissa figured she had four more hours of daylight before the cold winter air became her next worst enemy.

Moving more slowly now, the fever ravaging her body, Marissa fought off the rising delirium so familiar to her. She was more than aware of the need for her to keep a clear head, and she was equally aware of what might happen if she didn't. Two lives were depending on her to fight off the heat that burned her brain and baked her eyes, and she wasn't about to fail them.

As she fought her way through the forest, Marissa looked up and saw her father. He was waving to her as he always did before he left for work in the morning.

"Oh Lord," she said under her whistling, wheezing breath. "Not now, please not now." Stopping in her tracks, Marissa closed her eyes and inhaled slowly. She was burning up. Taking some snow in her hand, she wiped it on her face. The cold felt so good she lay down on her back and closed her eyes. She knew her father wasn't there; she knew she was losing the battle against her delirium. If she could not control the fever, she would lose her senses, and that would be the end of all three of them.

Closing her eyes, Marissa thought about the time she and Elsa sat in the snow and made angels and snow-women. She thought back to the time she and Josef had a snowball fight that ended when Mr. Liebowitz was smacked on his bald head with an errant snowball. The cold had a different feel to it then. Now, it was a cold

155

comfort; a way of combating the heat rampaging through her system.

"Get up, Mari," Elsa was saying to her. But Marissa could not open her eyes, nor could she respond. Suddenly, Elsa was not Elsa, but was Fritzi. Fritzi was screaming something in her face as a beard grew from his chin.

"Get up, you coward! Don't die on me now!" Marissa heard a voice from far away that sounded much like her own.

Opening her eyes, Marissa did not know where she was. The sun was not where it was when she lay down, and there were two tall shadows looming over her. Was it Fritzi? Elsa? Her Papa?

Rising shakily to her feet, Marissa tried to focus her blurred vision on the two men in front of her.

When she stood, her head did not pound as before, but to her surprise, the sun was well below where it was when she lay down. Looking at the two tall soldiers standing before her, Marissa slowly reached out and touched one.

"You are real," she said in Polish, more to herself than to them.

The touched soldier smiled. Turning to his friend, he translated her words from Polish to Russian.

"I have two friends in the woods. They are waiting for me to come back with help."

"Are these friends from the camp as well?"

Marissa nodded and looked down at her own torn prison clothes. "Yes. One of them was shot. She will need medical attention right away."

The Russian nodded and did not translate to his partner.

Looking for the trail markers she had made along the way with her bayonet, Marissa ran through the snow until she spotted the snow-covered log.

"Katya! Yvonne! It is Mari! I have come back with help!"

Pushing the branches away, Katya climbed out and hugged Marissa. When she saw the Russian uniforms, she did not move. "Mari, are you sure you know what you're doing?"

Marissa nodded, feeling the fever slowly return. "How can they be worse than what we've been through?"

Katya nodded and turned back to help the Russians pull Yvonne from under the log.

"How is she?"

"Not good. She needs a doctor soon."

Marissa watched as the two soldiers chattered to each other in Russian.

"Be careful," Katya cautioned in Russian. "It's her left shoulder. Be careful, not too fast, slowly . . ."

Marissa put her arm around Katya's shoulder. "Easy, Katya. They will take good care of her now."

Katya nodded, but said something else in Russian to one of the soldiers.

"Katya, perhaps it is you who should be careful."

"What do you mean?"

Marissa smiled. "Perhaps you have more feelings for Yvonne than you are willing to admit. Maybe you . . . enjoyed being with her?"

"Marissa!" Katya harrumphed. "Have you no shame?" Katya lowered her voice.

"I have two eyes. I see what is going on here. You need not confess to me if you do not wish."

"Maybe you are experiencing more delirium."

Marissa grinned, feeling the fever peek out at her again. "Maybe, but I don't think so."

As the soldiers bandaged Yvonne's wound, Marissa felt her head get heavy, and the sweat from her fever break the surface. She had felt this before and knew just what it meant.

"Katya?"

"Yes?"

"I'm sorry . . . I don't think . . . I can go any further." Falling to her knees, Marissa wavered a moment before landing face first in the snow.

"They both need a hospital," Katya said as the two soldiers scooped up the two frail women as if they were children.

Stepping next to the soldiers, Katya smiled. "Does this mean I have to walk?"

Chapter Forty-Two

Elsa cleared her throat. "I must tell you, I always envisioned leaving Auschwitz with Mari by my side. I was more than frightened to leave without her. So many things were happening so fast. One by one, I watched the women of my barracks climb into transportation vehicles until only a few of us remained. During that time, many people still died. Keep in mind, there were thousands of us to be removed. I chose to stay, in the hopes that Mari would show up somewhere. This delay is probably what kept us separated for so long after liberation."

Elsa was one of the last prisoners to leave Auschwitz. She went through every new pile of bodies, searched the entire compound a dozen times, and even took her one and only glimpse of the crematoriums. Still, there was no sign of Marissa, Katya, or Yvonne.

"It is time to leave this hell," one woman said, laying her hand on Elsa's shoulder. "Your friend went with my friend Hilde." She explained, shaking her head sadly, "Hilde was found in the showers when they removed the bodies. I'm sorry."

"I will not believe she is dead until I see her body."

"Perhaps it is best that you don't."

"No. Until someone can prove to me that she is dead, I will believe she is alive."

Elsa stayed until the final truckload of prisoners was taken away. Once she climbed aboard the truck, Elsa did not look back. Behind her was nothing but death, destruction, and misery. Looking ahead was all she had now. In her heart, she knew Marissa had made it. Maybe she was stronger than Elsa hoped. Maybe she was actually capable of running through the woods without getting killed. Wherever Marissa was and whatever she was doing, Elsa knew one thing was certain: Marissa Kowalski was alive.

Chapter Forty-Three

"Like so many thousands of displaced, I spent the next two months searching for information as to Mari's whereabouts. I had already known that Papa and Josef were gassed the morning we arrived, but I had it verified nonetheless. The Nazis were nothing if not fastidious in their notekeeping abilities.

"There was a small part of me that was glad Papa had not lived to suffer the hostile brutality. But Josef . . ." Elsa paused there and removed her glasses so she could wipe her eyes. "There is only one person I shed tears for now, and that is my Josef. I will always remember my little brother, and I will always grieve for the man he never got to be." Again, Elsa paused, steadying herself on the podium.

"Back and forth I travelled. Once I was released from the hospital, I began looking for her. From home to Auschwitz, to every hospital in between, always searching, looking for someone who had seen her alive. All of Poland was searching in those dreadful days after liberation. Close to three million Polish Jews had been killed, not to mention millions of other Poles, both civilian and military. We had lost our bodies, but not our spirits. As the German troops began pulling out, I felt my strength return.

"Still, so many families were separated, displaced, disconnected. Most of us did not know if our relatives were dead or alive. Like souls caught in the netherworld, we did not know whether to come or go, cry or laugh, wait or move on. It was the second form of hell on earth, but I was destined to live through it. After all, I had made it through Auschwitz. Now, all I had to do was discover whether or not my love had made it as well."

Finding some of her old friends still alive at home, Elsa stayed with them, washed dishes, and watched as Poland tried to rise out of the ashes. The Nazis had destroyed so much of the proud country, yet the Poles were determined to restore their nation and their national pride. And even though there were times when the rebuilding process seemed hopeless, they continued plugging away. Like so many other Polish Jews, she did not give up hope.

Elsa would work all night and ride the trains every day as she moved from town to town, looking for Marissa. Some days, when she was too weary to travel, she would simply sit in the town square, waiting, thinking, dreaming of seeing Marissa walking down the road. Every day, Elsa would search a different part of her world in hopes of finding Marissa.

Every day except Tuesdays.

On Tuesdays, she went to Tory's and sat on the porch watching them reconstruct the façade and the back where the shop had been broken into and looted.

"How does that look, Elsa?" Mr. Walesa would ask as he stood with paint brush in hand.

"A little darker would be better."

Mr. Walesa shook his head. "My wife said the same."

Every Tuesday, Elsa would read the paper, open a book, or write letters to some of the women she had spent a year with in the sewer. And when night fell and Mr. Walesa turned the outdoor light on, Elsa would pack her things up and trudge wearily back to the house, where she would wash dishes and occasionally whip up some delicious dessert as a gift of appreciation to her friends. She had little else to give.

"Elsa, my love, may I have a word with you?"

Elsa glanced up and saw Mrs. Walesa sitting in a chair across the patio. Rising, Elsa went over and sat across from her.

Reaching her old and withering hands out for Elsa to take, Mrs. Walesa smiled kindly. "Elsa, for the last few weeks, you have sat here, looking out like so many other lost souls, waiting for someone to return you don't even know is alive. Didn't you lose enough of your life already without spending it waiting?"

Elsa stared down at her hands which had just started healing. She wondered when the rest of her life would begin the same healing process.

Returning home had been a blessing and a disappointment. When she realized there was little for her to return to, roaming the villages gave her something to occupy her time. Her home looked different, so much ravaged by occupation and war. People looked different; worn, beaten, whipped nearly into submission. And life was a large, painful scab that seemed incapable of healing.

So much had changed since she was imprisoned. For one thing, she could no longer smell. It was a strange phenomenon that happened to many concentration camp survivors. Another oddity was that she could not sleep more than two or three hours a night. Every little sound was unfamiliar, and she would often wake up startled and afraid, half expecting the familiar search light to sweep across her body, half wondering when the cold night air would bite into her flesh. Then there was water. Some days, she showered two, maybe three, times a day, just letting the hot water run down her back. She didn't think she would ever get clean again. She didn't think life would ever be real again.

And always, there were the nightmares.

Sometimes, when she dreamt of the hangings, it would be Marissa dangling in the breeze. Other nightmares were of babies being butchered or women getting stomped to death. Death, it seemed, had even corrupted her dreams.

"She's alive, Mrs. Walesa. I don't know how I know that, but I do. And until someone proves differently, I will wait for her to return."

"But honey, if she were alive, don't you think she would have made it home by now?"

Elsa shrugged. "In Auschwitz, I learned to expect nothing and hope for everything. When Marissa left me, she was very sick. It's quite possible she's in a hospital somewhere. Maybe she has not healed yet. Maybe she is looking for me as well. Maybe—"

Mrs. Walesa reached across the table. "You cannot live your life on maybes."

Elsa knew differently. "That's where you're wrong, Mrs. Walesa. I just lived through a time when maybes were the rule and not the exception. Maybe I would live through the night, maybe I would have more food, maybe they would select me, or maybe they would send me to the Angel of Death. Maybe this was all one big nightmare." Elsa lowered her voice and looked down at her hands again. "You see, Mrs. Walesa, I understand maybes all too well."

Mrs. Walesa smiled gently and nodded. "And?"

"And maybe Marissa will come home to me."

Chapter Forty-Four

Marissa lapsed in and out of consciousness for weeks. Like so many other survivors, she was treated for dehydration, starvation, lice, worms, vitamin and mineral deficiencies, and exhaustion. On top of this, she had five broken ribs, one pinched vertebra, a damaged spleen, and a malfunctioning kidney. The doctors were amazed that she was even able to walk, let alone run from enemy fire.

Slowly opening one eye to the harsh glare of her hospital room, Marissa first focused on a familiar face staring down at her.

It was Katya.

"It's about time," Katya said, smiling. There was something very different about Katya's face. Was this a dream? Was she still lying in the snow, or had Katya and Yvonne vacated their hiding place a long time ago? Trying to focus, Marissa was puzzled. What was wrong with Katya's face? For a moment, Marissa stared up at the friendly face before her until she realized what it was.

Katya was wearing glasses.

"Where did you get those?" Marissa asked, slowly reaching up to touch Katya's soft cheek. There was a fullness to her cheek that had not been there before. Looking around the room, Marissa realized she was not in the forest, as she first suspected. She was in a hospital room, lying in a very warm, very comfortable bed. Standing next to the bed was a healthy looking little dwarf wearing a ridiculous smile on her face and glasses perched on her nose.

"Mari, do you have any idea how long it has been since you were brought here?"

Marissa shook her head. Hadn't she just slept a very long sleep and was now ready to be released from the hospital? Wasn't this the same day she had run away from enemy fire and collapsed in the snow at someone's feet? Someone . . . who were they? Weren't they—

"Almost six weeks."

The time did not register in Marissa's mind. "What?"

Taking Marissa's hand, Katya sat on the bed and held it firmly between her small hands. "We have been here for almost six weeks. You were a lot worse off than we imagined. The doctors said one more day and you would have died."

Marissa tried to sit up, but Katya gently pushed her back in the bed. "Six weeks? This is not possible." The sudden fear that she had slept part of her life away slammed hard into her.

Katya nodded. "I am afraid it is. They had to remove one of your kidneys and do something with your spleen. The fever kept you down for quite some time, and they weren't sure if you were going to lose the other kidney or not. I guess they stomped you pretty well." Katya bent over and kissed Marissa on the cheek. "But they say you'll be alright now."

Suddenly, all of her memories flooded back to her; their escape, their run through the woods, the two Russian soldiers, bullets flying everywhere, even into . . .

"Yvonne?" Marissa asked, trying to sit up. "Is she—"

Katya smiled. "She is fine. She stayed in here about a week before going home to see if any of her family survived. She tried to get in contact with people from your home, but no one answered. If Elsa went back to the bakery, no one has seen her."

Marissa sat back in the pillow. "Then she still does not know that I am alive?"

Katya shook her head. "Marissa, the world is even more upside down than it was before the war. Everyone is displaced. Families are searching for each other; people are going to villages that are no longer there; it is awful. Elsa is somewhere between Auschwitz and Bialystok, that much we know for sure."

Marissa sat up too quickly and felt the pain in her rib cage. "How?"

"Yvonne ran into others during her trip home. They said they saw Elsa on a train heading north."

"Then she is alive." It was not a question.

165

"Yes, my friend, and all we have to do is wait for you to get better, and we all shall find her."

Marissa's scarred eyebrow raised. "We?"

Katya smiled as the door to the hospital room opened and Yvonne walked in. Her hair had grown back quite a bit, and she had already put on several pounds to round out her large frame. Her smile seemed to walk through the door before she did, and so rare was it to see, that Marissa blinked twice to be sure it was really her.

Katya reached one hand out and took Yvonne's. "Marissa thinks we would let her find Elsa alone."

"I did not—"

Yvonne stepped over to the bed and touched Marissa's cheek with the back of her hand. Her left shoulder was lightly bandaged under her blouse and the yellow of her teeth was now an off-white.

"We made it this far together, Mari, we're not about to send you north alone."

Marissa closed her eyes and leaned back in her pillow. Its softness felt like nothing else she had ever experienced. "Six weeks?"

Katya nodded. "Long enough for us to put some weight on our bones. We were very concerned that you wouldn't make it through surgery. It took a while for you to regain your strength. Since then, we've just been waiting for you to get over the fever." Katya glanced over at Yvonne, who smiled warmly.

"And you, Kat, you never left our sides."

Blushing, Katya squeezed Marissa's hand. "Not until I was sure you were out of danger. Besides, time means nothing to me anymore. My family is dead—"

Yvonne suddenly put her arm around Katya. "I am her family now."

Marissa opened her eyes and smiled at the two of them, dwarf and giant, standing arm in arm. "I am very happy for you both."

"We want you to be happy for us, with us."

Marissa's head was beginning to hurt, and she didn't think she understood what Katya said. "What?"

Yvonne brushed a stray hair away from Marissa's face. "We are all we have, Mari. I am Katya's family and you are Elsa's. Except for each other, we are alone in this world. We want you to come with us."

"Come?"

Katya nodded eagerly. "To America. The Americans are much more sympathetic to us than most of Europe. No matter where we go here, we are looked upon as refugees. Yvonne has experienced this first hand. Besides, there's no telling what will happen now that the war is over."

"Many Jews and Eastern Europeans are already migrating. I hear America is a good place to pick up the pieces."

Marissa thought about this for a moment and nodded. Her pieces felt as if they had been scattered over the road for a tank to roll over. "Sounds wonderful."

"Then you'll think about it?"

"Of course. As soon as we find Elsa, we'll discuss it. When will you be leaving?"

"As soon as you're able."

Marissa held Yvonne's hand in one and Katya's hand in the other. Tragedy made strange bedfellows, she thought, peering down at the dwarf and then up at the tall Jew. These two women, having nothing in common with her except the pain they shared, had kept her alive. Not only had they helped her live, they understood the importance of staying together. Perhaps all four of them were meant to be together.

Marissa shook her head. It was beginning to pound. "You must forgive me."

"For what?"

"For not thanking you for all you two have done for me—"

Katya held up her tiny hand. "We could be thanking each other for hours. We're alive, Mari. Let's thank each other by celebrating that life together."

Feeling her head spin again, Marissa closed her eyes.

"Mari? Are you okay? Should we call the doctor?"

"No, no, I'm fine. It's all the excitement, that's all. After lying here and doing nothing for six weeks, my head doesn't know how to respond. I'll be okay."

Kissing Marissa's hand, Katya stood to leave. "You take all of the time you need, Mari.

"There's no hurry."

Yvonne bent over and kissed the top of Marissa's forehead and whispered, "We will tear the heavens and the earth apart to find her, Marissa. I promise you that." Opening the door, Yvonne smiled at Katya before walking out.

"You're in love with her, aren't you?" Marissa asked, sensing the warm glow surrounding the two women.

Katya pushed her glasses up the bridge of her nose. The beaten look she wore on her face in the camp was gone; in its place was the firm stare of a woman who knew she could now survive anything; a woman who had, remarkably enough, found love in hell.

"I don't know when it happened, but yes, yes I am."

Marissa closed her eyes and grinned. "She is a fine woman."

"Yes, she is. She saved our lives in those woods. She risked her own to keep us alive. It was then that I understood the role she played in the camp. Before that, Elsa's words about her fell on deaf ears. But now I understand. Yvonne is the reason we're alive."

"You don't think what you feel for her is gratitude then?"

A tint of pink covered Katya's cheeks. "Oh no, Mari. I felt something for her even before you became sick. She scared me so because she brought out these feelings in me that I didn't know what to do with. Watching Elsa love you helped me understand what was happening to me."

"So you slept with her because you wanted to?"

Katya bowed her head. "Not really. At first, I did it to help you. Then, whenever she touched me or held me, I knew that I was there because I wanted to be."

Marissa reached out for Katya's hand. "I'm glad. She cares for you very much."

"Yes, she does. You should have seen how happy she was to see me when she returned from home. She hugged me like she thought I might get away. That's when I was sure of her feelings for me. That's when I knew that I didn't want to be without her. This was a very lonely place for me with her gone and you in and out of fever. There were days . . .," Katya's eyes brimmed with tears.

Marissa reached out and grabbed Katya's other hand.

"There were days when I sat here and talked to you and prayed that she would come back to us. I did not realize how I was used to having her near me, even if she was playing the Kapo role. When she went home, I was scared she wouldn't come back."

"But she loves you."

"And I don't doubt that. But, Mari, you don't know what it's like out there now. People everywhere are trying to piece their lives back together with scraps of what used to be. I did not know if she would get home and realize that was where she needed to be. I simply did not know."

"But she came back."

Katya grinned. "She came through that door, Mari, and swept me up in the air, crushing me to her chest, saying that she would never leave me again. I believe her now."

Squeezing both of Katya's hands, Marissa pulled her to the bed. For a long, quiet moment, the two women looked at each other in a light other than the frightening pallor of the camp. Memories that were seared into their minds floated hauntingly past as they shared this moment together, and for the first time, Marissa realized what a beautiful little woman Katya was.

"I owe you my life, Katya."

"No one owes anyone anything when one has survived what we have. No one can take that away from us, Mari. The four of us survived because we relied on each other to get through the gates of hell and back to earth."

"We make quite an interesting little quartet, don't we?"

Katya nodded. "Indeed, we do. And don't you worry. We'll find Elsa, and when we do, life for us will begin again." Katya glanced at the clock. "Rest now. In the

169

morning, we'll see about transportation north in the days to come."

Marissa squeezed her hands tightly. "She does not know that we are alive. She could be anywhere. Her grief could have borne her far away."

Katya shook her head. "The rail systems are bogged down, and I don't believe she will just up and leave Poland. If I know your Elsa, she may well still be looking for us."

Marissa thought about this a moment and nodded. "I know her well enough to know she would want to see my body before she believed I was dead. No piece of paper will convince her otherwise."

"The Russians liberated Auschwitz some time close to when we were in the woods; she may know that we have escaped. Don't shortchange her, my friend. Elsa is a very resourceful woman. If she believes you to be alive, she is waiting for you somewhere."

A picture lit up in Marissa's mind. "And I know where."

Watching Katya walk to the door, Marissa smiled. It was odd seeing her in normal clothing.

"Then we will go there as soon as transportation is arranged."

Marissa nodded. "Then we'll go home?"

"If that's where you'd like."

Marissa hadn't thought of home in over a year. Home was a foreign place separated from her by barbed wire, machine guns, and too much space. Besides, what, exactly, was home if there were no relatives or loved ones with which to share it?

Closing her eyes, Marissa thought of home. Home wasn't a place. It was wherever she, Elsa, and their two companions hung their hearts.

Chapter Forty-Five

Watching the trains pull in and out of the station, Marissa held Katya's and Yvonne's hands. "Then it's settled. You two will go to Warsaw and see if there is any information on Elsa and her family as well as track down the brother of my friend Stefanie Sukova. There is an awful lot you can find out there. We'll meet in Bialystok in a week."

Katya pulled Marissa closer. "And you're sure you won't need us to help look for Elsa?"

Marissa looked down at Katya's eager face. It had been almost three months since they left Auschwitz, and Katya had blossomed into an independent, strong woman.

"I know where she is, Katya. The question is whether or not she's stayed there, or if she is running around Poland looking for us."

Yvonne stepped up and lightly touched Marissa's shoulder. "We are willing to wait, Mari. The war is over, and we have our lives to rebuild. Katya and I will go with you if you'd like."

Marissa smiled warmly. "We have waited long enough, don't you think? I cannot ask anymore of you than I already have. Take care of business in Warsaw and meet me at this address in a week or so." Marissa pulled out a slip of paper from her pocket and handed it to Katya.

Taking the paper, Katya flung her arms around Marissa's neck. "I am going to miss you terribly, Mari. But if being separated for a week will get us to America sooner, then so be it."

"Good. Then you'll go to Warsaw?"

Yvonne nodded. "This is what's best. We must get out of Poland soon, before postwar complications set in. Who knows how the rest of Europe feels about the Jews now? I do not intend on staying here to find out."

Taking both of Marissa's hands, Katya turned to her. There, in a frozen moment in time, the two women stood, feeling a connection few could ever truly comprehend. There were so many emotions, so many words left unsaid as they smiled gently into each other's face. The scars of their experience would never truly heal. They could start a new life in America, but they would forever be reminded of the days and nights when it appeared their life struggles would soon be over.

"You are a wonderful friend, Katya," Marissa said quietly. "I will miss you very much."

Katya pulled Marissa to her and hugged her tightly. "But not for long, I hope."

Stepping up to them, Yvonne handed Marissa a tiny box. "This is to ensure that you have no troubles along the way."

Opening the box, Marissa stared down at a pair of gold cuff links, a gold chain, and three gold rings with stones of various colors.

"What's this?"

"One day, when my father and I were hunting out behind our home, he bent down and dug a hole by the tree we always stopped at for lunch. He told me that he was saving the family's fortune for when the Nazis came and took everything away. That day, Mari, my father buried all of my mother's jewels, his money, and anything else of value that we had."

Marissa closed the box. "I cannot take this."

Yvonne pushed the box back to her. "Of course you can."

"But it is all you have left of your family."

"No, Mari. What I have left of my family is in here." Yvonne pointed to her heart. "No one can take that away from me. These things are just metal. They hold no sentimental value for me. I would rather you use them to find Elsa and book passage to America. That would make me happiest."

Marissa stared down at the glittering contents. She did not know what to say.

"Mari, I am wearing my mother's wedding ring. The rest means nothing to me."

Looking up from the box, Marissa wiped the tears from her eyes. "You are so generous."

"Not generous, my friend, grateful. We looked out for each other in Auschwitz. I see no reason that has to stop simply because we are free."

Free.

The word held a mystical quality for Marissa, who had not yet felt the full extent of her freedom. What was this freedom, anyway, if she couldn't share it with Elsa?

Katya pushed her glasses up on her nose. "Please, Mari, take them. Take them and find Elsa. There is nothing for any of us here except painful memories and emptiness."

Yvonne nodded. "The Jews are little better off now than before the war. The Polish nationalists still hate us, the Czechs are running us out of Czechoslovakia, who knows what is in store for us here?"

"That's right. So you take those in case you need fast money. Yvonne has the rest of the money to book passage to America."

As the conductor called for her train, Marissa snapped the box shut and dropped it in her pocket. "Then, America it is."

Yvonne and Katya smiled to each other. The conductor blew again.

"I must go, but it is so much harder to leave than I imagined. You are all I have right now." A thin line of fear ran down Marissa's spine.

"We all will have more, Mari. Just don't be afraid of finding it." Hugging Marissa in her powerful arms, Yvonne stepped back.

"Oh, Katya," Marissa sighed, pulling her to her chest and pressing her face into her. "I have gotten so used to seeing you every day I don't remember what life is like without you." Pulling away, Marissa cupped Katya's chin in her hand. "Thank you, for everything. If there is anything I can do—"

"There is." Katya smiled. "Don't ever have your tattoo removed."

Marissa looked down at her number. How many nights had she lay in bed and wondered if number 21060 would live to see freedom? She remembered Stef talking about staying alive so that others could know what had really happened. At one time, after she first entered Auschwitz, Marissa thought the first thing she would do would be to have it removed. But now . . . now she thought otherwise.

"Never. When Stefanie Sukova was alive, she told me she wanted to live to tell of the things we'd seen. That role is mine now, and it is exactly what I intend to do."

The conductor blew his final whistle.

"I must really go."

Hugging Katya and Yvonne for what she hoped was not the last time, Marissa stepped into the train. "Take good care of each other," she said as the train slowly pulled out.

"Wait for us, Mari. You and Elsa wait for us."

As their figures faded in the distance, Marissa promised herself that that was just what she was going to do.

Chapter Forty-Six

When the train pulled into the station, Marissa was already standing at the door. The ride was pleasant, but the countryside had drastically changed. Ravaged by war, the towns and villages were often in ruins, and people who once milled around the streets were nowhere to be seen. There was a hauntedness about Poland now—an eerie quiet that rose from the surface like a silent scream. The hustle and bustle of village life was replaced by slow-moving and often tentative actions, as if the people really weren't sure the ghettos were no longer operative.

At every stop, there were billboards posted with the names and whereabouts of lost family members. Marissa had already sent word to Stefanie's family in Czechoslovakia that she had died. Whether or not the family received her message would remain a mystery forever. In Warsaw, Yvonne and Katya would do the same once more, just in case.

That was one of the hardest adjustments to make now that the war was over. Just how did one go about returning life back to some semblance of normalcy? There was no way to be sure that anyone would ever receive a message or that any family was in the vicinity of where they came. For survivors of the concentration camps, life was one constant question mark.

Stepping off the train, Marissa started for the billboard and then stopped. She did not want her hopes to be dashed if there wasn't a note for her fluttering among the others. Besides, there was plenty of time for the billboard. Now, she had to go where she most suspected Elsa to be. She had to go to the place she knew Elsa must be waiting.

And, it was no coincidence that it was Tuesday.

Walking through the town, Marissa managed to spot a few familiar faces who were trying to rebuild their own lives. Many waved her over, but she did not have time to chat yet. There would be plenty of time for idle reminiscence, but now was not the time. Nothing short of God's angels could keep her from Tory's now. If she could have run, she would have.

Turning the final corner, down through the open marketplace that used to hold hundreds of shoppers, Marissa saw the top of Tory's. Just the sight of it made her heart quicken and her palms sweat. As the hedges surrounding Tory's came into sight, Marissa saw Mr. Walesa hammering away at his new sign.

Her heart beating rapidly beneath her chest as she neared, Marissa swallowed back her anticipation and wiped the sweat off her lips with the back of her hand. For just beyond the hedges, with her head bent down and her hand curled around a mug, was a woman staring intensely at something in her other hand.

All alone she sat, with her back to the hedges and to Marissa, who walked up to them and peered over.

For a long, tenuous moment, Marissa studied the short, boyish haircut around the soft curve of the neck. She gazed gently at the long fingers around the mug and the soft, almost childish way she cradled it in her hand. From this angle, she could see the dark eyebrows and the handsome curve of her cheek as she continued her steady stare at the object in her other hand. In this moment, with Elsa looking so vibrant and alive, Marissa could hardly believe that they had ever lived through the hell of Auschwitz. The sun on Elsa's face and the rose color about her cheeks reminded Marissa of the days long before war plunged its ugly dagger into their lives, changing them forever. Seeing her now, looking so peaceful and well, brought tears to Marissa's eyes and choked her throat. After all of her rehearsed daydreams about what she would say on this day, Marissa Kowalski found herself speechless.

What does one say when your dreams come true?

Then, as if sensing her nearness, Elsa looked sideways, out into the street, as if looking for Marissa. As her profile came into view, Marissa felt her knees give.

It was definitely Elsa.

176

Still staring out into the street, Elsa's eyes seemed searching, not of the street, but through time. Her eyebrows were furrowed, and she kept glancing at whatever it was she held in her hand. There was a power to that thing she now clenched in her palm. It seemed to give Elsa a strength that made her sit upright and dare the world to challenge her again. It was that same strength of character Marissa had seen from her in the camp; the same pain-induced self-possessedness Elsa displayed all throughout their ordeal.

Again, Marissa opened her mouth to speak, to say something that would alleviate Elsa's obvious pain, but the words would not come. Her heart raced, her palms were sweaty, and her tongue was thick in her mouth, yet Marissa could not speak. She could see the words she longed to say, but she could not find a way to push them from her mouth. Maybe she had fantasized of this moment so often, she did not know how to make it real.

"How does it look now, Elsa?"

Marissa started. While her own words were lost to her, it shocked her to hear other's.

"Very nice. It's coming along well."

Her voice. Her beautiful, even, tender voice. Hearing her speak, hearing her words for the first time, gave Marissa the courage she needed to speak.

Exhaling loudly and licking her lips, Marissa finally spoke.

"I knew you would be here," she said barely above a whisper.

Elsa did not move. Her mug, poised in the air at her lips, did not move. Elsa didn't blink, did not even breathe. She was afraid that the voice she longed to hear all these months might just be in her own head; afraid that, in her desperation to find Marissa, she was creating her dream in her own mind. Not turning around, not even breathing, Elsa waited.

"You knew I was alive, didn't you?"

Lowering the mug to the table, Elsa still did not turn around.

"Turn around and look at me, Sweetness. I am here."

At hearing Marissa's pet name for her, Elsa swung around in the chair and peered over the hedges.

"Mari! It really is you!" Running through the patio, knocking tables and chairs out of her way, Elsa flew into Marissa's arms.

"I knew you were alive! I knew!" Hugging her so hard it hurt, Elsa kissed her neck.

"My Sweetness," Marissa said, feeling the tears well up in her eyes as she clutched Elsa's back. Never had her hugs felt better, never could she have anticipated the spread of warmth that went through her body at this moment. It was as if her broken spirit and sore body healed at her touch, sending the pain and misery buried deep within her away to some other shell.

Closing her eyes and just feeling Elsa's body in her arms, two tears ran down Marissa's cheeks. This was better than any of her best fantasies; this was heaven.

Drawing slowly away, Elsa took Marissa's face in her hands and gazed for a long, quiet minute into her eyes. "It is you. I knew you would come. I knew you did not leave me." Running her fingers over Marissa's face, Elsa kissed her cheeks, her lips, her eyes, and her nose before holding her again. "I knew."

Brushing away the tears, Marissa nodded. "I would have come sooner, but I have been in the hospital all this time."

Elsa turned from Marissa and waved to Mr. Walesa. "Mr. Walesa, look! Marissa has come home!"

"Thank the Lord!" Mr. Walesa said, climbing off his ladder and running into the house to tell his wife.

"Oh, Mari, I never doubted you were alive." Taking Marissa's hands, Elsa brought them to her lips and kissed each one.

Marissa smiled and kissed her lightly on the cheek. "I promised you. You know I have never broken a promise to you."

Elsa nodded. "I know. But you came so awfully close. Are you still ill? Can I get you anything?"

"Only you, my love. You are all I need now." Pulling Elsa to her, Marissa kissed her on the mouth. "I have missed you so."

Returning her kiss, Elsa whispered, "I never gave up, Mari. I never stopped believing."

Marissa reached up and touched the two-inch long hair on the back of Elsa's head. She looked so much healthier since Marissa last saw her. Like Yvonne and Katya, she had put back some of her lost weight, her hair had grown, and her face was clean and vibrant. With the exception of her short hair, Elsa appeared very much as she did the day they prepared to go to Auschwitz.

At least, that was how she appeared on the outside. Marissa knew only too well, the scars that would forever remain on the inside.

"But how did you know? When you last saw us—"

Looking down at her closed hand, Elsa slowly opened it to reveal the silver cross Stefanie had given to Marissa. "I found this on the outskirts of the woods. I knew you had escaped the showers; I just didn't know if you outran the bullets. When I found this, my hopes were buffeted by a tiny breeze. But it was enough. It was . . . oh, Mari, it was awful." Burying her head in Marissa's shoulder, Elsa wept. Whether it was from joy or sorrow or relief, Marissa did not know.

"I'm sure it was."

"Everyone kept telling me to go on with my life, but I couldn't. With Papa gone and Josef . . . you are all I have. I could not possibly give up on you."

Marissa held her tightly and kissed the top of her head. "And you didn't."

"No, I didn't. I couldn't any more than I could just stop breathing. But I was so scared . . ."

Gently pulling away, Marissa wiped Elsa's tears. "It must have been awful, not knowing whether to go or stay, look or wait. I tried to send word, Sweetness. I would have done anything to spare you more grief."

Elsa looked into Marissa's eyes and nodded. "I know you would have. But that's not important. You're here now and that's all that matters. That's all that ever mattered." Lightly kissing Marissa's mouth, Elsa blinked away more tears. "I had hoped . . .," Elsa stammered, feeling more tears roll down her face, "that Kat and—"

"She is. She and Yvonne are both alive." Marissa reached out and wiped Elsa's tears. "We escaped the showers by fleeing into the woods. It was our last, desperate gamble. None of us wanted to die like sheep led to the slaughter. So we killed the guards, took a gun, and ran into the woods. Yvonne saved us by shooting the soldiers who came after us. She was shot keeping Katya and me alive."

"And you say she is alright?"

Marissa smiled. "Very much so."

"And my Katya? She is well also?" It was more than Elsa had dared hope for.

"Yes."

Elsa's face lit up. "Why is she not with you?"

"She and Yvonne have gone to Warsaw to get information on you and Stefanie's brother who lived in Poland, and to get the necessary things in order for us to leave for Amer—"

"Yvonne?" The light in Elsa's face brightened as if turned up a notch. "They are still together?"

Marissa smiled and nodded. "They love each other very much. Somewhere along the way, they discovered each other. It's very cute."

A slow smile slid its way across Elsa's face. "I am not surprised. Yvonne is a good woman. She loves Katya very much."

"Indeed. Enough to offer her life as a sacrifice twice in one hour."

"Yvonne loved Katya for a long time. It was that love which kept Katya alive in the camp."

Marissa nodded. "They wanted to come, but we did not know if you would be here. Warsaw, I hear, is the best place to find information about lost loved ones."

Elsa shrugged. "I understand that it's dumb luck if one rejoins their family unless they all go home. That's why I decided to stay here."

Marissa lightly brushed her finger across Elsa's eyebrow. "Are you determined to stay in Poland and rebuild our lives here?"

"Weren't you about to say we are going to America?"

Pulling Elsa to her, Marissa held her hands and leaned over to kiss her forehead. "Yvonne and Katya want us to join them, Elsa. Who knows what Europe holds for the Jews? I know it's a long way away, and that you might want—"

"Yes."

Marissa's one eyebrow raised. "Yes?"

Throwing her arms around Marissa's neck, Elsa laughed. "Yes! Yes! Yes! I will go anywhere with you, my love. Anywhere."

"I love you so much, Elsa." Kissing her tenderly at first and then harder, Marissa crushed her closer, uncaring whether or not Mr. Walesa was looking. Nothing superficial mattered to her anymore. All that mattered was what she had in her arms this very moment.

"Mari, what will poor Mr. Walesa think?" Elsa asked, playfully fanning herself. It was the first real smile Marissa had seen on her face in over a year.

Tossing her head back, Marissa roared. "Who cares? Who cares now what the world thinks of us, my love? We are alive, we have each other, and we are free."

"Free." Elsa whispered the word as if in doing so would take it from them.

"Yes, my love, free."

Freedom never felt so good.

Chapter Forty-Seven

"Some months later, Yvonne, Katya, Elsa, and I arrived in America, having bought passage with the jewelry Yvonne had given us and other funds we scrounged along the way. Elsa and Kat's reunion was one of the most touching and inspiring sights I have ever witnessed as they stood looking at each other through eyes cleansed of pain, anguish, and sorrow. Yvonne and I could merely look on as the two of them held each other as they had done so many nights in the freezing cold and damp hostility of Auschwitz.

"The four of us eventually made our way to Southern California, where Yvonne was able to get some minor acting roles, and I got a job sewing costumes for the booming movie industry." Marissa paused here and smiled into Elsa's face.

"And I," Elsa continued, "opened a bakery with the money Yvonne and Marissa made, and Katya and I worked every day. As the years went on, more and more survivors came to America. And each year, we hold a vigil in the United States as well as take our annual trip to Auschwitz.

"Yvonne and Katya are both retired now, and they live in the upstairs portion of our home. We have been a family since our arrival in the United States, and I'm sure we will continue to be until our final days."

Marissa stepped back to the mike and inhaled slowly. "I was finally able to locate Stefanie's brother on one of our annual trips, and I related her story to him. As we spoke, I could see Stefanie's face in his, and I could hear her voice as he spoke. I relayed to him how daring and brave his sister was and how she met death with a dignity and poise few ever mustered. When I showed him this cross and told him what a strong and resilient sister he had, he broke down and wept. And as he and I held each other and cried, I remembered her telling me to tell the world. Her words came back to me as if she had just spoken them to me.

"I remembered my promise to her. That promise is why we are here today. In memory of the Stefanies and Claudias, the Papas and the Josefs, who were not as fortunate as we were, we *thank you for listening to our triumphs and hope you will share our story with others so the world never forgets."*

Holding her necklace off her chest, Marissa stood proud and erect. "It is only in the remembering that we can be sure it never happens again. So remember . . . remember."

Epilogue

When I first started telling others about *Tory's Tuesday*, everyone kept asking if I was Jewish; as if the atrocities and the horrible nature of their imprisonment was of interest only to other Jews; as if the Jews were the only victims of the relentless killing machine.

I am not Jewish, but I am a History teacher who understands the importance of remembering. If we allow ourselves to forget, however briefly, what cruelty humankind is capable of inflicting upon itself, then who will be next? Who will be hounded, imprisoned, enslaved, or burned at the stake? Which of us will find ourselves face to face with a society which tolerates little or no divergence from its archaic standards? If we forget what happened to 10 million Europeans, how can we possibly move forward enough to ensure it never happens again?

Tory's Tuesday is my humble attempt to remind us all of how easily we can turn on ourselves. Only by keeping alive the memories of those lost to the ovens or showers, can we hope to prevent such crimes against humanity from happening again.

"Remember . . . remember."

Linda Kay Silva

About the Author

Linda Kay Silva was born and raised in Danville, California, where she still resides. She has been teaching Middle School English and History for the past eight years. Last year, her first novel, *Taken By Storm*, was released by Paradigm Publishing. She has three sequels to *Taken By Storm* being prepared for publication. The second book in the series will be released in 1993.

Publishing
Company

A paradigm is one's perception of reality which is generally formed out of one's experiences and cultural traditions. We firmly believe that the paradigms of mainstream society need to be continually critiqued and challenged, and new paradigms created. This work has generally been best accomplished by communities of diversity which have been placed on the fringes of mainstream society because of their diversity. However, their voices have been silenced by inaccessability to traditional publishing avenues.

Therefore, Paradigm Publishing has joined the network of small presses dedicated to providing diverse communities with access to being published and being heard. We encourage these communities to tell their own stories, thereby empowering themselves and society by the creation of new paradigms which are inclusive of diversity.

Other Books Published by Paradigm Publishing:

Practicing Eternity by Carol Givens / L. Diane Fortier, Lesbian Nonfiction/Health, ISBN 0-9628595-2-4 $10.95

Taken By Storm by Linda Kay Silva, Lesbian Mystery, ISBN 0-9628595-1-6 $8.95

Expenses by Penny S. Lorio, Lesbian Fiction / Romance, ISBN 0-9628595-0-8 $8.95

Available at your local bookstore or order direct: Paradigm Publishing, P.O. Box 3877, San Diego, CA 92163. Add 15% postage and handling. CA residents add 7.75% sales tax.